LIZIWE

LIZIWE

A Novel

Monde Nkasawe

PARTRIDGE
A Penguin Random House Company

Print information available on the last page.

To order additional copies of this book, contact
Toll Free 0800 990 914 (South Africa)
+44 20 3014 3997 (outside South Africa)
orders.africa@partridgepublishing.com

www.partridgepublishing.com/africa

Contents

Dedication vii

About the Author ix

Prologue xiii

SECTION ONE 1

    Unease at Dawn 3

    The Mind Numbing Music 10

    The Deathly Procession 18

    Mother Where Are You 25

    About Nonzame 29

SECTION TWO 35

    A New Existence 37

    These Are My Mother's Children 45

    The Silly Meeting 59

SECTION THREE 67

    The Walk to Fate 69

    The Beckoning City Lights 74

    A Prayer for the Road 78

SECTION FOUR 83

    The Children at the Gate........................... 85

    Meeting Father's Other Woman 93

SECTION FIVE 107

    The Kindness of Strangers.......................109

    Beginning of a New Beginning................ 114

    Silence at the House of the Le Rouxs..................... 118

    Affairs Set in Order 127

SECTION SIX 137

    A Passage of Time...................................139

    The News..146

    Manyawuza is in Town............................ 151

    Going Home 156

Epilogue..167

List of Characters 175

Dedication

This book is dedicated to my family, for the wonderful support and inspiration. I have also received support from a number of people, all urging me to continue to write, for which I'm eternally grateful. I am particularly grateful to Dikeledi Molatoli for reading and giving feedback on the manuscript as it was being developed. Above all, this book is dedicated to all who refuse to live in a comfort zone; to all who reject the idea that they have arrived; to the restless mind to which what is, is not enough.

About the Author

Monde Nkasawe was born on the 22nd of March in 1966 in the then Transkei part of the Eastern Cape, at a town called Cofimvaba. He was educated in the rural schools of the Eastern Cape, including Ncorha Junior Secondary School, Main Mission Junior Secondary School, Sabatha High School, and Falo High School. After obtaining his matric certificate he left for Cape Town where he enrolled for a Bachelor of Arts degree at the University of Cape Town. He left UCT in 1995, having obtained a BA Honours in History, and joined the University of the Western of the Cape for a Master of Arts degree in History, which he completed in 1997. In 2004 he continued with his studies, enrolling at Wits University for a second master's degree – a Master of Management degree in the field of Public and Development Management, which he completed in 2006. Monde Nkasawe is the author of three other books - a poetry anthology entitled 'Journey of the Heart', as well as two novels, 'The Death of Nowongile' and 'Pieces', all published by Kwarts.'

Free yourself
Push the encircling horizon away,
and with all strength in you
Pound and hammer at the encaging sky!

Prologue

"I must sit down. I can't go on anymore now. My knees are so sore! *Nkosi yam, haz'uba Yintoni na le!*" said Mandla, speaking to himself, with a tired sigh, as he made his way towards a row of Vaal Maseru busses in downtown Johannesburg. It was now just after ten o'clock in the morning, and he had been up since dawn. The transit from Dobsonville to Johannesburg, which had started with walking for about a kilometre to catch a taxi, had taken its toll on him.

Now, moving slowly, with his head bowed and his face a picture of consternation, he muttered, "I need to take my tablets. God! This pain is killing me!" He was talking to himself, totally oblivious to the fact that there were hundreds of other people milling around him. He could feel the pain, all over his body, with every step he took feeling like a thousand sharp knives mercilessly piercing his body.

The conductor of one of the busses, a stout, big bellied fellow in green overalls, saw him limping along, and when he came closer to the door of the bus, he stepped forward and said, "My brother, here let me help you. You're traveling with us, right?" Mandla slowly nodded his head as he handed the man his bag. With tired eyes, he looked at the bus conductor, and figured the man couldn't be older than 45 years. Ordinarily, Mandla would have bargained with him - to try and force a ticket concession out of him. But today he didn't have the energy for that.

"Good. Call me Tshangisa. Brother, you sure don't look well", again the conductor said, gleefully looking at Mandla, up and down. He too was sizing Mandla up, already making a mental calculation of his bottom line.

"Are you sure you want to come aboard?" he asked, feigning concern. Mandla again nodded his head without saying anything. He so desperately wanted to tell this man to mind his own business! But alas, all he could manage was a feeble gesture for him to hurry things up.

The bus conductor then took out his ticket book, and said, giving Mandla a mischievous look, "Well, it's your funeral. You had better pay now then. Where are you going to?"

"Cofimvaba", Mandla replied, almost whispering. "Cofimvaba, you say", the conductor said, scribbling something on his book. "It will be R150" he said nonchalantly. Mandla took out his leather wallet and selected a few shiny ten rand bills and handed these to the eager bus conductor.

"Well then my brother, you can climb aboard, that is, if you don't mind waiting. The bus to Cofimvaba and Mthatha is still at the depot, being serviced. You can wait in this bus for now. You will be offloaded to yours in about two hours", the conductor said, flashing a smile and waving Mandla towards the steps at the doorway of the transit bus.

"Oh boy", said Mandla as he struggled to climb up the steps on the doorway of the bus. "There was a time when this was easy!" he said ruefully. He sat alone at the backseat of the bus, although he was not actually alone in the bus - but he very well was as good as, so engrossed was he in his own miserable world.

There was a buzz at the bus terminus, which he completely blocked out. This included bus engines which were constantly revving. Many people were also playing mbaqanga and reggae music in their tape recorders as if in competition about who had the most powerful speakers. Others were moving up and down the rows of busses selling a range of goodies, from bananas, vetkoeks, very fat pork meat, and cardbury sweets.

Mandla had not said this aloud to anyone, but he knew deep down that this was a one way journey - a fact confirmed, subconsciously perhaps, by the single ticket he bought from the conductor just before he boarded the bus. Unlike previous times, when he would have about four suitcases with him, today he was travelling light, with just one medium sized metal case and a brown backpack like leather bag. He did not have the energy to bring with him all his other possessions, which were pretty much left in a clutter in his backyard shack in Dobsonville. His illness had forced him to make a hasty departure. Today he was leaving Egoli for the last time, enroute to his hometown of Cofimvaba, not as an old man going on retirement, but as a sick and broken young man headed to likely expiry.

His decision to go home a few months before he was expected had been sudden, though not entirely unforeseeable, especially after breaking up with Mavis, his girlfriend of many years. With Mavis he had a nine year old child – a girl named Lizeka, and possibly a three year old boy named Phikolomzi. But after the breakup, which was sparked by his discovery that Mavis had been cheating on him by Mxolisi, who too was quite possibly the father to

Phikolomzi, everything just seemed to be going downhill, with no prospects of improvement. Not only did Mavis kick him out of her house, ostensibly for his own many infidelities, but also for refusing to leave his wife for her, she wasted no time in moving in with a new boyfriend.

'That rat!' Mandla swore under his breath as he sat alone in the bus, feeling cold even though it was blazingly hot outside. He felt utterly helpless and defeated. He could not explain what was going on in his body. At first it was the flu, which would come and go. But, within a very short space of time, that progressed to coughing, sweating at night, and then diarrhoea. Although it was not yet noticeable, he was also losing weight.

All this deterioration of his health happened very quickly - more or less within six months. During this time he had been to see a number of 'people', which was to say he had visited various sangomas in Dobsonville and at various other places within Soweto. He had of course also been to a few doctors, all of whom prescribed TB drugs. But Mandla, as a general rule, didn't believe in Western doctors. He wanted people who would tell him the nature and source of his illness, without first asking him to describe and say where the pain was. Traditional healers would throw bones and then 'see' what was wrong with him!

Alas, up to this point there had been no respite. Instead his illness began to also negatively affect his work at the Durban Deep mine in Roodepoort, leading to him being medically boarded by the mine management.

As the bus was filling up with fellow 'Transkeians' Mandla felt not only sick but apprehensive. The boisterous chatter among fellow passengers, with all of them still very excited by the birth of the new 'nation' of Transkei, did not help him to take his mind off things. Instead, he thought about Nonzame, his wife, at home, and the children. The last sangoma he had been to, had said, "Go to your wife. She will take better care of you."

But he felt guilty. He had not written to Nonzame in a little over a year now. He had not informed her that he was sick. He had not told her that he had been laid off work, and he definitely did not tell her that he was today enroute to her.

Now he was going to her, fully expecting her to burden herself with his illness. It was a thought that compounded his discomfort. What right did he have of expecting to be taken care of by someone whom he had ignored, to put it mildly? He asked himself, fidgeting and beginning to sweat. He took a deep sigh, and then he closed his eyes. He was in pain, and the closer it got to sunset the more incessant his cough became.

For a moment he thought about the children. It was a thought that brought both a smile and a grimace. He loved his children, but he doubted if they knew that. How could they? He asked himself exasperatedly. How could they indeed, when they could only see him once a year? As it was, only Liziwe, his eldest daughter could claim to know him. But even that he doubted. Otherwise, to Tembisa and to Ntando, he was as good as a total stranger.

Again he sighed. He could feel himself wanting to cry. Just then, he heard the bus cranking up, and with one final check of all the passengers aboard, the bus driver started the journey home.

SECTION ONE

UNEASE AT DAWN

Silence. Unusual. Normally there would always be something stirring even in the dead of night, be it dogs barking, a voice or footsteps of somebody already up or never slept, the rustling sound of trees, or even the sound of cows ruminating – but never nothing, such as was today. "Something is wrong", Liziwe heard her own voice, sounding as if it was speaking independently of her. She wasn't sure if she actually said this, or if it wasn't a dream. It didn't matter. She was now awake, and panicking about something she couldn't yet say what it was.

She looked around, trying to see if she could make out anything. But she couldn't see a thing. She stretched her arm out from underneath her blankets and felt for a match, which she kept under her pillow, and then lit a homemade paraffin lamp, which was also within easy reach. Again, she cast a quick eye around the room. This time she could see the silhouettes of Tembisa and Ntando, who were still asleep on the mattress across the room, and she could hear them snoring.

She looked at the time – it was just a few minutes past four o'clock in the morning. The old winding clock had been wrong before, and she wasn't sure if it wasn't now. It was one of those many trinkets and things brought home by her father whenever he came home for the holidays, and it worked on a very simple principle - if you had forgotten to wind it, then you didn't have time for that day!

She pulled the curtain aside slightly and looked through the single pane window. It was pitch dark, and she couldn't see a thing. She decided to go back to sleep – convincing herself that it was still too early to wake up, and she blew out the paraffin lamp and covered herself fully with the blankets.

But just as she was willing herself to sleep some more, she heard the familiar and irritating noise, eerily breaking the uncomfortable silence that had been up to this point. There they were, without fail, waking everybody up. Liziwe heard them going, '*Kurukuguuu! Kurukuguuu!*' 'God! Do these roosters really have to do this?! *Tyhini Thiza!*' She swore and fumed as she tried desperately to bury herself deep into her blankets, trying to muffle the intrusive sound of the crowing roosters. But to no avail. The bloody things were programmed by nature to do this.

But her irritation was unusual, perhaps a harbinger of the air of unease she was feeling. Certainly, Liziwe, the eleven year old first born daughter of Mandla and Nonzame Ncadana, was used to waking up very early in the morning. It was pretty much her usual regime. Everyday, without exception, even on weekends and on public holidays, she would wake up at around this time. In fact, there had been several times in the past when she would dare the roosters to catch her sleeping!

So used was she to this routine, that by now she had completely internalized the reality that her day would end, not at sunset, but when her body no longer could cope with the day's chores. It was a routine that had been drilled into her by her mother - that everyday she must wake up early to make fire; boil water; cook porridge; go and fetch water from the fountain; do the laundry; stamp or grind mealies; apply cow dung to all the floors of their three huts; do everything else in between, including running errands in the village; and going to the trading store for groceries.

On school days these chores would be spaced out such that some would be done in the morning and others in the afternoon – after school. By now Liziwe – and her teachers at Mcuncuzo Primary School had given up on her ever getting to school on time. The principal of the school, Mrs Zou Banzi, had even given an instruction to the school staff to just accept that the Ncadana children would always be late, and so they should spare rod, fearing that anymore beating would do more harm than good.

As it was, if anyone would ask how Liziwe's day was like, all she would say in reply was that all days were alike. Sometimes it would rain, drenching every item of clothing, and turning the hard ground into slippery, foot clogging mud. Sometimes it was cold as hell, with every person that talks looking like they are chain smoking. Sometimes it would be dark and overcast, a gloom carrying the real possibility that lightening might strike, and yet also portending life-giving downpours. Sometimes there would be a fresh breezy wind blowing about, giving relief from a blazingly hot summer sun. Be that whatever it was, the truth was, for Liziwe in particular, and at the Ncadana household in general, none of it mattered. Time, seasons, the day's weather, and circumstance, were irrelevant. The sun rose and set, monotonously exchanging each day with each night.

Today was a Monday, the 3rd of December 1979, and regardless of the drama provided by the irritating orchestra of the roosters, it was a day that did not hold any promise that it would be any different, with the exception that it marked the beginning of the week. Like all the others before it, it was just a normal a day. Liziwe had to wake up, as she always did, and start preparing hot water for her parents, who at this time were still asleep in the big hut situated on the far left of their three rondavel home.

It was therefore strange that she would feel tired and lazy to wake up today. Whereas usually she would just jump out of bed, today she was experiencing a hitherto unknown lingering need to sleep some more. Although she couldn't say what it was exactly, she felt that something was amiss. For one thing, with the exception of the noise made by the roosters, there was unusual silence in the house. Her father's constant coughing, which was particularly worse in the evenings and in early mornings, was today conspicuously not there anymore.

Even more strange was the silence of her mother's voice, which always prodded and directed her through her chores, with statements like, "Liziwe, hurry up, we don't have all day!" or "Liziwe, wake up girl, wake up! *Ayikhw' inkomo yobuthongo*! There's no reward for sleeping!" There was silence.

Liziwe briefly wondered if they had gone to some place perhaps. But that was unlikely – she would have known, because, whenever her mother had go to some place, the list of things to do in her absence grew exponentially.

Still, Liziwe knew that, whatever the situation was with her parents, she could not linger in bed for long. Even though she had not heard her voice this morning, she still expected her mother to walk through the door anytime from now, to wake them up - she, her seven year old sister Tembisa, and even her five year old brother, Ntando. Liziwe figured she could wait for that to happen, but she decided not to, reckoning that since she was awake already, there was no point in pretending otherwise.

She looked again through the window. Even though it was actually summer, she felt a bit of a chill as soon as she took her arms out of the blankets. But she knew that the cold she felt was not going to last – that this was just a morning thing. The little radio had predicted an afternoon scorcher, with temperatures expected to soar above thirty degrees Celsius. It was going to be hot, and in the afternoon there was a real possibility of thunderstorms.

Thinking about the thunderstorms somehow injected a sense of urgency for her to get up and get started with the day's work. She had seen the dangerous effects of this kind of weather at her own village of Mcuncuzo, and had been warned by her mother on numerous occasions, that weather like this always produced serious disasters, with mud-built homes collapsing, being swept away or the huts with thatched roofs being struck by lightning.

Having procrastinated for about ten minutes, Liziwe finally managed to pull herself out of 'bed'. In no time she was fully dressed, which was to say she was wearing her old, and now off colour brown crimplene slacks. She called this item of her clothing, 'slegs' – as in s-legs. And because she felt a bit chilly, she also put on her old and oversized cardigan jersey which she called '*nam' ndiyatitsha*'. If you asked her why she called her jersey by this name, she probably would not know, except that it was a popular fashion item among the teachers at her school. Underneath the jersey she was wearing a t-shirt, and, as always, she was bare feet. As it happened, the only shoes she had were a pair of black school idlers, and she was strictly forbidden to wear them around the house.

Liziwe neatly folded her blankets, with the dexterity of somebody who had done this all her life, and rolled, and then pushed her mattress against the wall. After that, she woke everybody in the room up, including the five year old Ntando.

This early in the morning, poor Ntando was moody and cranky. But he woke up as soon as he heard Liziwe's voice calling him. He was not crying, but he was not playful either. In general, he was just not a morning person, and he would always be peeved at people telling him to leave his warm blankets and go outside to wee. But, in spite of himself, he had become accustomed to being woken up at this time, even if begrudgingly, and to then just sit on the pile of folded blankets against the wall, to watch his elder sisters as they went about their morning chores.

As soon as she was sure that indeed everybody was up, Liziwe asked Tembisa to fill a size ten three-legged black pot with water. She then went outside to make fire, using a combination of sweet thorn tree logs and dry cow dung cakes, while Tembisa was busy scooping dishfuls of water from an enamel bucket into the big black pot. When Tembisa was done, she called out to Liziwe to come inside.

"Liz, I'm done, the pot is full, but the water is finished", she said as soon as Liziwe came through the door. Liziwe curtly responded, saying, "It's fine, it's fine. But we'll have to go fetch water from the fountain, now." Tembisa just nodded her head and did not say anything. Liziwe continued, "Come Tee, let's drag this pot out to the fire."

In between grunts and with a lot of water being spilt all along the way to the fireplace outside, the two siblings managed to drag and place the pot of water on the fire. When they were done, and with the fire now holding, they grabbed two enamel water buckets and rushed to the fountain, to fetch water, before it got muddied by the cows. It was still dark outside, but Liziwe and Tembisa were not the only ones out. Many people from the neighbourhood had the same idea – to beat the cows to the water.

Tembisa was of course too small to carry a full bucket of water all by herself. She had not yet mastered the skill of balancing water laden buckets and other heavy objects on her small head. But Liziwe insisted that she comes with to the fountain and to carry, even if it was half a bucket of water. It was as if she desperately wanted Tembisa to learn this - and as soon as possible. She wanted to make sure that her siblings, especially Tembisa, but Ntando too at a later stage, quickly picks up the routine, in order to ensure that the load of chores in the house was shared equally.

THE MIND NUMBING MUSIC

"Hey Liziwe! Come girl, come. Let's go, time is up already! *Iinkomo ziyawagxobha lamanzi!*" Liziwe heard the call coming from MamQoco, one of the women in the village. She was well aware of MamQoco's daily habit of calling out for her every time she passes by the house on her way to the fountain. "I'm coming, I'm coming *sisi, ndiyeza ngoku!*" Liziwe yelled back as she and Tembisa grabbed buckets and followed MamQoco to the fountain.

For a while after this, Liziwe and Tembisa became preoccupied with fetching water from the fountain, which was about three hundred meters away from her home. Together with many young married women in the village, including MamQoco, Liziwe and Tembisa made several trips to the fountain, filling up every container in the house with water. The fact that she and her sister Tembisa were the only children awake at this time was also something the older women at the fountain were fascinated about. They all wanted to chat with Liziwe, asking about her sick father and how her mother was. They would also talk pejoratively about their own children, who they said, unlike Liziwe, were lazy and couldn't be bothered with any chores around the house, let alone wake up this early in the morning.

These women were older than Liziwe, needless to say. Most of them were 'newly-weds' or '*oMakoti*' as Liziwe called them, and some were the same age as her mother, between thirty and thirty five years old. Yet they all spoke to her as if she's their age. And because she could read, some of them often invited her to come to their homes, either to read or to write letters from and to their husbands, who were, almost in every instance, in the gold mines of Egoli. Because of this, Liziwe had intimate knowledge of the issues each of them had in their marriage, their fears, especially about the health, education and general wellbeing of their children, and their concerns about not having enough money to afford some the things they needed.

At just a few minutes after five in the morning, about an hour since Liziwe and her siblings had woken up, the sun was still not up yet, even though all the darkness of the previous night had almost completely receded. The little chill Liziwe felt earlier when she was struggling to wake up, had also all but faded, yielding to a hot day in prospect.

Already Liziwe and Tembisa were done with the first part of their chores. There was enough water in the house, and even the water they put on the fire was now hot enough for people to wash.

Liziwe briefly felt a slight sense of relief. The chat with the women at the fountain had helped her to momentarily forget about the concerns she had for her parents earlier when she was waking up. But the lingering feeling of unease returned as soon as she thought about going to the big hut where her parents were still asleep. She became concerned once more about the fact that her mother had still not woken up. She was tempted to go to the big hut to check what was going on. But she resisted the temptation, figuring that she would soon find that out anyway when she brings hot water to them.

Tembisa, in her own precocious way, sensed that there was something not quite alright with Liziwe today, as she asked with childlike concern, "Liz, are you alright? You seem unwell."

Liziwe replied, with her face feigning a puzzled look, "Ag there's nothing wrong with me Tee, just tired maybe, but nothing really."

Tembisa didn't say anything else. She just shook her head in disbelief and wondered off to chat with Ntando, who also was not helping matters, as he kept asking for his mother. All Liziwe would say to him is, "Aw come now Ntandos, she's still asleep, but she's coming anytime now." Still, Ntando would remain nonplussed.

But even as she denied it, Liziwe knew deep inside that Tembisa's observation was correct. She was not feeling OK, and it worried her that little Tembisa could pick up on it. But what exactly did she pick up on? Really what was it that was bothering her so? She asked herself keenly. So her mother had not yet woken up, so what? It was not as if she had never overslept before, though admittedly very seldom. Liziwe argued with herself, as she paused momentarily, trying to think.

Perhaps it was something she ate? But she was not in any physical pain or discomfort. So what then was bringing her down? Perhaps it was just stuff at home. But what stuff would that be? Of course, other than just doing house chores as she knew them, or as directed by her mother, Liziwe had never really paid much attention to any troubles at home. Her mother was there to take care of all grown up stuff about the house.

Yet there she was today, downcast and thinking about stuff, some of which was about her father. She was well aware that, quite apart from it being a habit, lately the need to wake up very early in the morning was also necessitated by the fact that her father was sick and bedridden. For quite some time now, his illness was a situation they were desperately trying to cope with as a family.

In fact as far as she knew, her father had been like this, at least, since the day when they brought him from the hospital, about three months ago, during which time, he was lying in bed, which was to say he was on a mattress, unable to move or do anything normal with his body. Even though he could eat by himself, and could still wash most of his own body, it was a struggle, at the end of which he would always be very tired. As time went by, Liziwe observed her father progressively becoming worse, to an extent that he no longer had any energy left in him. He had no appetite for food, and everything he ate coming out on both ends almost immediately.

At times the nurses from the nearby clinic, doing their routine rounds around the village, would visit and give him an injection and a cocktail of TB related tablets. Sometimes, members of the church, especially the women of *umanyano* after their Thursday sessions, would also come and conduct a prayer service at the house.

Liziwe did not know exactly what was wrong with her father. But she had become accustomed to hearing him cough constantly and seemingly with a certain measure of pain. She saw him changing from a bulky person, with broad shoulders and well developed body muscles, to an emaciated and helpless thing, almost overnight.

She had seen her mother doing everything she could to get him to hospitals. She listened to her mother's frustrations at how the hospital was treating her father. They were unable to help him, they said, and so he had to be brought home to be looked after by his family. Liziwe could not understand this, that a hospital could actually declare itself unable to provide treatment to a sick person. As a result, her mother, had now taken it upon herself to feed and clean her husband every day.

With a slight grimace, Liziwe thought about how she had accepted, albeit not without her mother's stern instructions, that one of her duties in the morning would henceforth also include throwing away her father's 'chamber'. This chamber, which Liziwe called '*tshemba*', was her father's night soil bucket, and Liziwe hated it! Yet without being expressly told, she knew, and had accepted that this was one task she would not push down to Tembisa, much less Ntando.

But just as she thought about her father's poor condition, Liziwe could not help but also think about something that she had thus far resisted to dwell on. But she heard her own voice saying out loud what she had been thinking and noticing, '*Eshee! Kanti ke nomama uyagula bonanje!*' Today, in her dejected state, she realized that she had in fact also noticed, albeit without paying much attention to it, that lately, her mother too had become sick.

Even though she had never been hospitalized or anything, but Liziwe had noted that her mother had slowed down in a somewhat dramatic fashion, and that she too, just like her father, had lost a great deal of weight and her gait had become strained, as if she had suddenly grown old. Of course Liziwe did not know her mother's age, except that she was not 'an old woman'. That she was actually thirty three years was information she was not privy to as a child.

Even more concerning for Liziwe, in recent days, her mother had shown signs of being disinterested in directing and partaking in house chores. The more her father's illness progressed to a worse stage, the more whatever was left of her mother's energy seemed to be visibly drained.

But sick as she was, Liziwe knew that her mother would always make a point of waking up very early in the morning, and would then go to the middle hut to wake the children up, and to ask them to make fire for the morning tea and to order them to go fetch water from the fountain. Today, for the first time, she did not do this. As the children, they woke up all by themselves, and were not guided by anyone in all the things they had to do thereafter.

Liziwe tried to put these concerns aside, figuring that whatever it was that had kept her mother from waking up, it would not prevent her from doing what needed to be done at that moment. She tried to inject more energy into the chores they were doing, and in no time she and Tembisa started to move up and down, darting from one room to the next, mainly between the middle and the small hut, doing their chores, with little Ntando following them about.

Today of course, even though it was a Monday, school was not a factor, as schools were already closed for the summer holidays. In fact Liziwe was aware that it was a few weeks to Christmas. Yet, even though at her age she would be expected to be fanatical about the magic of Christmas, the truth was she had no particular concept of, or attachment to it. At her house Christmas was just not the thing, and even today, there was nothing in the house even remotely resembling a Christmas spirit – well, except for the sounds coming from the radio that was sitting snuggly on a sideboard shelf among a row of shiny enamel plates.

Even this early, the small Tempest transistor radio, which she called 'the FM' or the 'wireless', pronouncing it '*wayilesi*', was doing a countdown, urging people to beat the rush to the stores in town. The stupid thing, as she at times called it, seemed to be stuck. It was constantly playing this mind numbing Christmas music over and over again. By now she had memorized the lyrics of the Boney M song, '*By the Rivers of Babylon*", without even meaning to!

The monotony of Christmas songs was only broken at the top of each hour by brief news bulletins, the content of which was mainly about a re-narration of the latest speech of the Paramount Chief; exploits of the South African Defence Force in engaging the 'enemy' in the Caprivi Strip in the northern border of 'South West Africa' and south of Angola; the latest number of 'terrorists' arrested by the South African Police; events surrounding the signing of the Lancaster House Agreement by ZANU-PF and ZAPU-PF on the one side, and the government of Ian Smith on the other, which was said to be paving the way for the independence of 'Rhodesia' the following year; the latest condemnation of the 'communist' and 'terrorist' inspired calls for the release of Nelson Mandela; and the new deadly disease attacking the immune system in human beings, and for which it was said there was no cure.

To Liziwe, all of this was just background ambient noise. She didn't care much for the music, and she didn't care for the radio chatter either, and even today, she had switched the radio on, more out of habit than any particular interest in its programming. She loved playing and fiddling with the radio, and she was always very curious about the workings of this little contraption, even thinking that there were people inside it! It was her father's, and in truth, she and her siblings were prohibited even from touching it.

But Liziwe switched it on at any time and had lately not been reprimanded by her father for doing this. When used 'properly' by its owner, it only did three things, namely to listen to the broadcast of obituaries, the news, and the 'story'. Otherwise it stayed silent to preserve the Eveready batteries with which it was powered. And Liziwe knew the drill, that when the batteries are old, they were kept alive by baking them in the sun, either on the roof of one of the huts or by perching them on one of the stones that made the kraal wall. But in recent times, her father had not seemed to care about any of this anymore.

THE DEATHLY PROCESSION

"He didn't say 'sharp-sharp'. Dad didn't say 'sharp-sharp'!" Liziwe said, almost yelling, and looking at Tembisa, but not really talking to her. "And mom – it's like she's not even there!" Little Tembisa was puzzled about the cause of this outburst, to say the least. She didn't know what to make of it, and so she just looked at her sister inquisitively, but said nothing. The last she checked, Liziwe had gone to the big hut to serve tea and porridge to their parents. But quite what transpired there, Tembisa had no idea.

Of course, by now it was midmorning. The village of Mcuncuzo was abuzz, with people herding their livestock to the grazing fields, young women in a seemingly endless procession to and from the fountain to fetch water, and some headed either to the trading store or to town for groceries. Even though the sun was still rising, it was already hot.

The heaviness in Liziwe's heart had also somewhat lifted – not so much because she had decided to mellow down. But the frenetic set of activities she and Tembisa were involved in since dawn just had not allowed for anymore gloominess to set in.

In fact, by seven in the morning, Liziwe was done serving her parents. Working closely with Tembisa, with

Ntando playing either in the middle hut or outside near the fire place, part of what she had to do was firstly to give her parents two washing basins filled with hot water. Her mother always insisted that nobody must touch food in the morning without at least washing their hands if they could not yet wash their full bodies.

In quick succession, after giving her parents water to wash, she then served them tea. Her mother liked her tea scalding and strong. Two full scoops of Teaspoon Tea leaves into a one litre kettle, mixed with a generous amount of condensed milk, and then allowed to percolate on embers for a while, always did the trick. Later Liziwe served them with sour porridge made of fermented maize meal.

At the same time she also dished porridge for Ntando and Tembisa, and then for herself. It was while they were sitting down to eat their porridge that Liziwe just burst out about the seemingly unresponsive behaviour of their parents. She recalled that when she went to the big hut to serve her parents their water, tea and then porridge, she had noticed that her father was still sick – not that she had expected his situation to be any different. But she noted that today he did not even move to acknowledge being served, which he always did by either waving his hands, as if to say 'put it there, I'll deal with it later', or by giving a 'sharp-sharp' sign. Today he was silent, and still, and did not acknowledge anything - neither the water, the tea, nor the porridge.

Later, when Liziwe went back to the big hut to collect the tea cups, she noticed that her father's washing water had not been used, and it was now cold. The tea and the porridge had also not been touched, and were now also cold. She did note however that her mother, unlike her father, did use the washing water, even though it was merely to wipe her face and her hands. But she also did not drink the tea, and did not touch the porridge.

More puzzlingly, Liziwe had also noted that her mother was not talking, not to her and not to anybody else either. She just wasn't saying anything! She was expecting her to ask her usual 'check list' type questions, such as, 'Did you go fetch water from the fountain?' 'Did you make your beds?' 'Did Ntando eat anything?' 'Did Tembisa have a change of clothes?' But no, she did not ask about Ntando. She did not ask about Tembisa, and she did not give any of her usual instructions about what other chores must be done. She was just quiet.

Puzzled and confused, again Liziwe decided to ignore this, and to pay attention on the little things she still had to do, which included throwing her mother's dirty water away, and collecting the unused tea cups for washing in the other room. There was also a pile of washing that needed to be done, and there was mealies that still needed to be stumped in time for cooking by at least midday.

But just as she was trying to again put her concerns aside, Liziwe saw Manyawuza coming through the gate. Ever since her father arrived sick from Gauteng, Manyawuza had made a habit of visiting the house every day, and today was no exception. In fact the fifty five year old Nothembile Guluza, known to everybody in the village by her clan name of Manyawuza, was the closest neighbour to the Ncadana household. She lived alone in her two rondavel house.

On the first day when Mandla arrived home from Johannesburg, Manyawuza came just to greet, and to get her share of the provision of goodies from Johannesburg, which she called '*padkos*'. Every 'new one' arriving from the mines of Egoli was expected to bring home padkos, which invariably consisted of things like scones with jam and raisons, 'home' baked bread, sweets, and lots of meat – all kinds of meat including pork, beef, mutton and chicken.

But Mandla's arrival was unusual. Not only was there no *padkos,* he was actually sick, and it looked, to Manyawuza, like Nonzame, Liziwe's mother, would need her support to cope. And so Manyawuza made it her business to wake up every day and come to check up on how Mandla was doing. But more than that, as Liziwe very well knew, perhaps it was out of a need for company, that Manyawuza was always visible in the Ncadana house. She and Nonzame always accompanied each other to events in the village and spent a great deal of time together. And so when Liziwe saw her coming through the gate today, she was not unexpected.

"Hello Liziwe", Manyawuza said in her usual enthusiastic fashion as soon as she saw Liziwe, "is everybody alright today?" she asked.

Stopping in midstride for a moment to acknowledge Manyawuza, Liziwe replied, "Yes mama everybody is fine, well sort of anyway."

"What do you mean?" Manyawuza asked with unmistakable concern in her voice.

Liziwe replied, "Tata did not use his washing water this morning. He did not drink his tea and he did not eat his porridge. And mama barely touched hers."

"*Hayi bo! Inoba kutheni*?!" exclaimed Manyawuza, "I had better go in and see what is going on. Ntando and Tembisa are alright though, are they?" she asked.

"Yes mama they are", Liziwe replied, just as Manyawuza was entering the big hut to check on her parents.

Momentarily putting Manyawuza out of her mind, Liziwe went inside the small unoccupied hut on the far right of the house. At the centre of the room there was a pile of dirty laundry, covered by a dirty white linen sheet. She grabbed at one end of the sheet and dragged the whole pile outside to a patch of green grass just in front of the middle hut. She wanted to put the laundry on this patch of grass, spread it out and then sort it.

Even though she was fully engrossed in this, Liziwe noticed Manyawuza coming out of the big hut that had her parents. Her face was now sombre, and there was a sense of urgency about her steps as she walked past Liziwe without even looking at her. 'Strange', said Liziwe quietly to herself, and again momentarily cast aside Manyawuza's behaviour from her mind, and returned to the task of sorting the dirty laundry.

But about ten minutes later, Liziwe again noticed Manyawuza coming back through the gate, this time with three elderly AmaQwathi women, whom she knew as Mamanci, Soyintombi, and Nodanile. There was also one old man with them, and this was Madevu, who too was a senior member of the AmaQwathi clan. Liziwe stopped sorting the washing, and for a moment she looked at these people as they walked past her, again appearing not to even notice her.

Instinctively she knew that something was wrong. She knew from experience that these people did not make social calls, certainly not at this time of the day. The only reason they would be here at this time is if there was home brewed beer – and there was none. And so the only other reason for them to come together like this was if there was something wrong.

She called out for Ntando and Tembisa and the three of them huddled around the spread-out dirty laundry, looking at the people passing by, to the big hut. But even before she could figure out what was happening, more elderly people were now coming through the gate, all of them members of the AmaQwathi clan, and they all seemed to know where they wanted to go, because even though she was sitting there in the open with her siblings, none of them was asking her anything.

"Liz, why are these people coming to our house?!" Tembisa asked, also sounding curious, and looking at Liziwe.

Without looking back at her, Liziwe replied, "I don't know Tee, but it looks like the whole of Mcuncuzo is coming here today!"

Still, a string of more people, a mixture of neighbours, friends and relatives from the AmaQwathi clan, started streaming through the gate and were headed to the big hut. All their faces were grim, and all of them were barely noticing Liziwe and her siblings as they huddled on the patch of green grass in front of the middle hut of their house.

At this point, Liziwe became even more curious and wanted to find out what was going on. She stood up, and at the same time said, looking at Tembisa, "Tee, look after Ntando. Don't go anywhere. I want to see what's going on in that room." Tembisa nodded her head and put her arms around Ntando.

Liziwe, walking slowly but determinedly, approached the big hut with her parents, and paused closer to the door, which was closed. She could hear the voices inside the hut. Someone was praying, and it was a man, probably one of the elderly men she'd seen coming through the gate. And then, as soon as the man had said 'amen', someone started to sing a church hymn, and then the door was opened.

Somehow the opening of the door startled Liziwe, and she was caught between wanting to run away, and entering the door. But Manyawuza, who was busy lighting candles and unfurling straw mats on the floor, and directing everybody to their places, saw her and immediately called for her to come in.

"Come in, come in Liziwe my child. Don't be afraid. You are old enough now to know these things", Manyawuza said. Cautiously, Liziwe entered the room, wondering all the same what 'these things' were. It was hot, and there were many people in the room, some of them were wiping their sweating brows with handkerchiefs, and all of them were looking at her. Even though she was not maintaining eye contact with any of them, she could feel their stares. Yet she was not afraid.

She looked around the room, panning the room with one head movement, and sure enough, she could see her father lying on the mattress and his body was covered in full, by a blue striped blanket - the kind used in hospitals and prisons. He was dead.

She froze. Liziwe had never seen a dead person before, yet she knew instinctively that her father was dead. Perhaps it was the atmosphere in the room, because, even though the room was full with people, still, it was eerily quiet and deferential. She did not say a word, and as if taking the cue from the adults around her, she just stared at the covered mound representing a lifeless body in front of her.

MOTHER WHERE ARE YOU

Liziwe stood there, in the middle of the room, surrounded by a roomful of elderly people. She was not crying, and her face was bland and betrayed no emotion. Even though this was her father, she felt no emotional connection with him. To be sure, she didn't hate him. But they had never been close. In fact, since he arrived two months ago he did not say anything to her – not even a hello. For the better part of her life, she had felt estranged from him. She didn't know why, nor was she sufficiently aware of her own detached attitude towards him. Her whole life – her thoughts and her dreams were completely dominated by her mother. Perhaps this had to do with the fact that her father was away from home for eleven months in a year, every year, and only came home in December. All she knew right at that moment was that looking at the lifeless form in front of her didn't fill her with any particular sense of loss.

As she was about to turn and head towards the door, she looked at her mother. She was sitting on one of the straw mats that had been prepared by Manyawuza. She was looking down, at her hands, as if studying her own palm prints. Liziwe looked at her, trying to make eye contact with her and to get her to notice her and maybe say something. But she didn't lift her head up, and she didn't say anything.

As she was proceeding towards the door, she heard the voice of Manyawuza calling her, and it jolted her to the reality that she was not alone in the room.

"Liziwe, my child, don't go just yet", Manyawuza said. "As you can see, your father is no more. It was not unexpected, you know…" she trailed, but continued after a brief pause, "We shall bring the rest of the children in as soon as possible so that they too can be told."

"No, not here. Not like this!" Liziwe snapped, her tiny frame suddenly shaking with anger. But just as suddenly as she said this, she quickly realized that she had committed an offence, and she put both of her hands on her mouth as if to prevent it from saying anymore improper things! She had heard her own voice, and was horrified at her own rasping tone.

Liziwe had been taught to respect people older than herself, and not to speak out of turn or raise her voice at an adult. Yet just now she did exactly that, almost yelling at Manyawuza, in front of people, for the suggestion that Ntando and Tembisa be brought into the room with their dead father.

As it happened, she needn't have worried. Manyawuza had also realized the error in what she had just said, realizing that the children would likely be traumatized more by the scene than by the news of the passing of their father. She recanted, saying, "You're right my child, we shall have to manage this differently." She looked at Liziwe, searching for confirmation or agreement. But she could see that this was one task Liziwe preferred to do herself, and so she said, "Perhaps on second thought, you tell them yourself then hey. How's that?"

Liziwe slowly nodded her head, and then turned around and left the room, leaving behind a slightly bemused and sorrowful lot of people behind, all looking at her with pitying and curious eyes. Once outside, she headed straight to the front of the middle hut where she had left Tembisa and Ntando.

They were clearly apprehensive. There had never been a death in the Ncadana household before, and even when the women of umanyano would come to conduct a church service for their sick father, it was always by prior arrangement with Nonzame. The congregation of this many people at their house today was having a dramatic effect, especially on little Ntando and Tembisa. Both of them didn't say anything, but both were looking at Liziwe searchingly.

"Tata is gone" said Liziwe, matter of factly, and as if she was talking to herself.

"Gone? Gone where?" Tembisa asked, bewildered.

"I mean, he is dead. That is why all these people are here", Liziwe said, again coolly, without looking at them.

There was silence. Tembisa had never heard of such a thing before, of a person being said to be 'dead'. After a while, Tembisa again asked, resignedly, "Now what?" Liziwe replied with a sigh, "I don't know. I guess there will be a funeral." As Tembisa was still trying to make sense of what she had just said, Liziwe continued, "Anyway", she said pointing at the pile of washing, "I don't think we can do this now. Come, let's take this washing back."

As they were once more dragging the pile of dirty laundry back to the small hut, little Ntando burst out crying. It was blood curdling stuff, as if he was hit by something very sharp or very hot. Liziwe dropped her end of the pile and rushed to him. In between hugging and trying to dry his eyes with her hands, she asked, "Ntandos, what happened?!"

Ntando replied, snorting and pulling back his tears, *"Ndifun' umam'm mna*! I want my mom! I want to go see my mom!" Again he screamed. Liziwe was frantic. She had always known Ntando to be a well behaved child who didn't throw a tantrum. As she tried to calm him down, wiping his tears and picking him up, Tembisa also started to cry, at first tears rolling down her cheeks, and then she started to convulse uncontrollably. Liziwe pulled the two of them together in a huddle, all the while talking to them, asking them to stop crying, telling them that it's gonna be fine. She did not realize that she too was crying.

Manyawuza heard Ntando's scream and came rushing out from the big hut. She could see immediately that the children were badly affected, and tried to do her best to calm them down. She took Ntando and held him against her chest and rushed inside the middle hut to get him a glass of water, all the while saying to him, "There, there my boy. *Thula mfana wam, thula.* You're a man maan, you shouldn't cry like this, hey. Are you hungry? Come on now, your sisters are going to give something to eat."

With desperation in her voice, and with her arms flailing, Liziwe asked Manyawuza, "MamNyawuza *kant' umama uphi*? What is wrong with her today?! Why can't she wake up? What's wrong with her?!"

Of course as far as Manyawuza was concerned, these questions were rhetorical, all caused by the pressure the children were filling at the moment. But nonetheless she responded, saying "I don't know my child. Perhaps the situation is too much for her, I don't know. Please be strong, and continue to look after the children, will you?"

ABOUT NONZAME

By nine o'clock in the morning, with the summer sun acting as if it had only the Ncadana household to focus on, everybody in Mcuncuzo was still coming to pay their last respects to Mandla. As the children were crying and wailing, not so much at the loss of their father, but clearly for the stress caused by their suddenly comatose mother, more people were still coming to the Ncadana household.

Manyawuza was busy. She was sweating profusely as she tried to coordinate the immediate logistics surrounding Mandla's death, which included making tea for the constant stream of mourners. As soon as she felt that the children were now calm enough, Manyawuza left to make a telephone call to the mortuary, to arrange for Mandla's body to be removed and taken to the mortuary. She knew that it would be a while before the mortuary would be able to come to Mcuncuzo, and therefore thought it wise to initiate the process of recovery of Mandla's remains early enough.

More worryingly for Manyawuza, she felt alone, like this tragedy was hers alone to handle. She felt Liziwe's desperation about the state of Nonzame, her mother, and quietly she prayed.

Of course, Manyawuza, perhaps more so than Liziwe and her siblings, was aware that Nonzame was also sick. Even though she did not know the full extent of it, Manyawuza knew that in fact Nonzame had been sick for some time but had been trying to hide it. She wanted to appear strong and in control, not only for the sake of the children. She also knew that, when Mandla came home from the mines two months ago, his situation would need her undivided attention. So she tried, in spite of how she truly felt, to be strong. Each time Manyawuza asked her how she was, or made an observation about how unwell she looked, all Nonzame would say is, *"Akukhonto wethu Nyawuza, kukudinwa nje."*

But she was sick. She had been to several doctors, in Cofimvaba, Engcobo and Mthatha. They all said she had TB, and prescribed a cocktail of tablets. But the last doctor she went to about a month ago, in Queenstown, took blood samples and after a while she was informed that it was not TB. It was the 'big disease', for which there was no cure. She was HIV/AIDS positive, and it was at full blown stage.

Today, as Manyawuza was doing her best to calm and placate Liziwe down, Nonzame, sitting on the straw mats alongside Mamanci, Soyintombi, and Nodanile, all of whom were Liziwe's relatives, was progressively becoming worse. It seemed the death of her husband had completely immobilized her and removed her ability to speak or do anything. She was just lying there motionless and staring into open space. Even as Manyawuza was making hasty arrangements for all the children to be informed about the death of their father, Nonzame was neither showing any interest, nor for that matter, any evidence that she was even aware of what was going on around her.

However, as it was, unbeknownst to Liziwe and Manyawuza, Nonzame had come under a heavy bout of flu the night before. Just before going to bed, she felt her legs sagging and as soon as she lay down for the night, she found, to her horror, that she did not have enough strength in her legs and could not stand up.

She tried to remain calm – even though she could feel herself beginning to panic about what possibly was going on in her body. Even though ordinarily she always tried to avoid taking sleeping pills, because she wanted to remain alert to anything that may be going on with Mandla at night, this time she felt that she'd be more sick if she didn't take anything to make her sleep.

When she woke up in the morning, at almost the same time that Liziwe and children were waking up in the other hut, all she could manage was to lift up her head. Otherwise the rest of her body was numb from her torso down to her legs. When she tried to call Liziwe, she found, to her horror, that she had lost her voice.

It was also around the same time when she heard Mandla doing what she thought was an unusually weak cough, followed by noises she thought were akin to convulsions, and then becoming silent. She knew instinctively that Mandla had in fact passed at that point. But she could not scream and inform the neighbours. When she saw Liziwe coming into the room about two hours later, bringing water, tea and porridge, she could not warn her that this was no longer necessary.

Now sitting there on the straw mats along the wall, unable to move or talk, she could only watch the commotion caused by the death of Mandla. And just like Liziwe, Mandla's lifeless body, still in the centre of the room waiting for the mortuary people to come and collect it, did not fill her with any particular sense of loss.

It had been two months since Mandla arrived home from Johannesburg, and in all that time they had not had time to discuss anything serious about their lives - not about their lives together as husband and wife, and not about their children. All they talked about in brief spells was how Mandla was feeling, where the pain was, whether it was better or worse than it was yesterday, and whether he would be able to eat anything at all. Nothing else.

Nonzame knew that what had killed Mandla was the same disease that had now so afflicted her. The doctors had confirmed it to her. That last doctor they went to in Queenstown, Dr Willis Schoeman was brutally frank with her, saying, in no uncertain terms, "You both have the same thing, and you got yours from him. Nothing can be done now. I wish you all the strength, and bless you."

And today as everybody was in shock and getting ready to start a week long process leading to the interring of Mandla's remains, Nonzame was feeling utterly helpless, and angry. She had seen Manyawuza trying her best to make light of the situation, by talking to her children and by leading the all the necessary logistics. And even though she appreciated this, being totally unable to do anything for her children increased her desperation. When she heard her children wailing outside the big hut, her heart ached, and she desperately wished that she could reach out to them. But alas, she couldn't.

But she was also very angry, at Mandla. She had tried her best to get Mandla to be well, so that he could be strong enough to answer some of the questions she had. She kept asking herself for example many questions, such as, 'Why was he so unfaithful to me? Why did he sleep around with those sick and cheap women at the mines? Why did he bring all this suffering to his own house, to his own children? Why did he infect me with this disease? If I die now, what will happen to my babies?!'

By midday, the people from the mortuary had not yet arrived. The heat in the big hut had become so unbearable that, the men had now left and were gathered in the open space near the kraal, while the women remained behind, mostly singing church hymns.

And then Nodanile, one of the women who were sitting on the straw mats with Nonzame, after quickly and expertly checking on Nonzame, stood up and walked outside to the group of men gathered near the kraal, and called out for Madevu, an old member of the clan of AmaQwathi, and said, "Mqwathi, *khaw'ngene Dikela*. I think you had better come inside. We are having a problem with Nonzame. I think she's dead."

SECTION TWO

SECTION TWO

A NEW EXISTENCE

Tuesday, the 11th of December 1979 - a hot summer day, with not a single cloud in the sky. Temperatures were predicted to reach alarming levels, at 42 degrees Celsius. But, hot as it was, it was nonetheless late into the ploughing season, and people were out and about tilling their fields. Although normally there would be long drought spells affecting Mcuncuzo and villages nearby, such as Mtyamde, Kwazulu, Kwasijula, Qombolo, Tsojana and many others, this year the rains were not scarce. In fact even today it was predicted that it would rain in the afternoon.

As the heat was climbing to predicted levels, everybody was in a rush to cover as much acreage as was possible. And so the subsistence maize fields on the outskirts of the village of Mcuncuzo were teeming with people and spans of oxen. You could hear the crackling sound of a sjambok goading the cows to pull the plough through what sometimes was rocky and hard soil. Everybody was calling out the name of their cow – all with fancy names such as, 'Zawulani, Blue Sky, Wazama', etc. And everybody knew that by about midday the cows would have to be rested for the day.

Yet, for all the heat in the world, it was all the same, just an ordinary day for the orphaned children of Ncadana.

Even though there had now been no reason for this, Liziwe had woken up at the same time as always, very early in the morning. By six o'clock in the morning, she and Tembisa had finished their water fetching trips to and from the fountain, and she was now busy preparing their morning porridge, just as she had always done.

Of course for the village of Mcuncuzo, the exception about today was that it was a little over a week since the tragic passing of Mandla Ncadana and his wife Nonzame. Their funeral had taken place three days ago, on Saturday, the 8th of December 1979. Prior to that, the funeral had been preceded by a series of meetings in the house, all coordinated by the old man Madevu, and most of them concerning various aspects pertaining to the management of the tragedy, including the funeral arrangements.

But by now, after these few but intense days, the Ncadana household was deserted. All the pots which were used to cook during the funeral were now clean - and the cutlery that had been borrowed by Manyawuza from the neighbourhood had all been washed and had been returned to its owners. For all intents and purposes, the people of Mcuncuzo had now moved on to other more pressing matters in the village, leaving the Ncadana siblings alone.

There was of course still some evidence of recent events. The neighbourhood dogs were still congregated in the front yard of the Ncadana household, yelping, barking and fighting among themselves for scraps. There was also still some leftover meat, a few loaves of home baked bread, as well as few grocery items. In her usual considerate manner, Manyawuza had insisted to the young women from the village who were cooking for the funeral, that some food be left for the children.

Now with Mandla and Nonzame dead and buried, their children were beginning to experience a new existence. For the first time in their lives, the eleven year old Liziwe, the seven year old Tembisa and the five year old Ntando were alone, at home, and in the world. Liziwe, as the eldest of the three children, became entrusted, by default, and by fate, with the task of looking after her siblings, and after her parents' house.

And much as she was not consciously planning to be a 'parent' over Tembisa and Ntando, she had already effectively assumed that role. Both Tembisa and Ntando, since the fateful morning when their mother would not wake up, were now looking at Liziwe for everything they otherwise would have asked from their mother. And today, as they were looking forward to yet another 'normal' day, filled with the usual routine of chores around the house, Tembisa, who had been unusually quiet all this time, suddenly asked, "Liz, so mom is really not coming back then, is she?" When she asked this question, Tembisa had been quietly sweeping the floor and then suddenly she stopped towards the centre of the room – and looked with appealing eyes at her sister.

Although Liziwe had not expected this question just at that moment, she was glad nonetheless, because she thought Tembisa was now finally coming to terms with the loss of their parents.

"No Tee, she's not. *Uhambile mntana'sekhaya*", Liziwe replied, tapping Tembisa gently on her shoulders. "Don't you worry though", she continued, looking away as she could feel tears welling in her eyes "we will be fine. I assure you, we will be fine. I'll see to it that we are fine!"

It was as if Liziwe knew, and accepted it implicitly, that from now onwards, it would be on her tiny shoulders that the future for the three of them would rest. Even though this was a situation which had taken effect immediately, without allowing her to come to terms with it, she seemed to have already internalized what her role would be from now onwards. It was as if she accepted the challenge, to either swim from the deep end – or drown.

But the full extent of this reality had not yet hit home equally among the children. Even as Tembisa was showing signs of accepting the situation, Ntando was still asking, "So when is mom and dad coming then?" - a question which Liziwe quickly learnt to either ignore and pretend she didn't hear, or answer simply by giving Ntando something to eat, to distract him.

Tembisa on the other hand was only now beginning to find her voice after a long and unusual spell of silence. Before today, she too had expected her mother to return. Yet with each passing day, her expectation had started to fade. Knowing Tembisa as she did, Liziwe had been expecting her to explode as soon as she realizes the finality of the loss, and she had silently wished that this would happen sooner.

For her own part, Liziwe kept thinking about what Manyawuza had said earlier, that she should "be strong, and take care of the children." In fact as she sat in their middle hut, helping Ntando with his porridge, Liziwe thought again about what Manyawuza had said. The responsibility to take care of the children was something she accepted without any reservations.

But it made her to think, perhaps more than she had ever done before, about the fact that she didn't have any relatives - at least none that she knew of or had interacted with to any degree worth a meaningful connection. She knew that her father's parents had long died – even before she was born, and both of her father's siblings were also dead. She knew too that from her father's side, there was the clan of AmaQwathi, all of whom had helped organize her parents' funeral. But as far as she was concerned, they were all strangers to her, and for that matter even if she knew some of them, as she knew old man Madevu and Nodanile, this was not enough a basis for a lasting emotional bond. From her mother's side, the story was pretty much the same. Her mother's parents had also long died, and she had never seen, and had not heard of any of her mother's siblings.

Liziwe suddenly felt bothered by her own reflective mood. All this thinking about having to take care of the children, made her to feel uneasy, as if suddenly realizing the magnitude of the task. She decided to go to the big hut.

Ever since her parents died, she had shied away from that room, fearing that it would revive the image of her dead parents in her head. The image of her father lying dead on a mattress and of her comatose mother was still fresh in her mind. Yet a part of her wanted to confirm once more that they were gone.

As she stood up to leave, she said, looking at Tembisa, "Tee, I'm going to the big hut. I want to sort out mom and dad's stuff. Start washing the dishes as soon as you're done eating, will you?" Tembisa was also curious about this stuff Liziwe wanted to sort out, but for the moment she just nodded her head.

As soon as Liziwe was inside the big hut, it occurred to her that she had never been to this room without a reason, which always was about a chore of some kind. She stood in the centre of the room, looking, first at where her father had been, and then at the spot where her mother died. She shook her head, trying to fend off a rush of tears, to no avail. With tears streaming down her cheeks, she blurted out words she didn't know where they came from, with her voice quivering with emotion:

"Mama, notata! Yintoni le nindenza yona? Nithi mandithini ngoku? Nithi mandibathini aba bantwana? I wish you'd told me that you were leaving! This, what you have done is not fair. What am I to do now? Where am going to get food for the house? What am I expected to do with Tembisa and Ntando? When both of you decide to leave us here alone like this, how do you expect us to live?!"

But just as suddenly as Liziwe said all this, she checked herself, realizing that she was in fact speaking to an empty space. She composed herself, wiping her eyes with her own bare hands, and again she looked around the room, this time focusing more attention on the spot where her mother had been. She started to think about her own relationship with her. She and her mother had a strong bond. Theirs wasn't a love based on spoiling or fawning, but on something akin to mutual respect. Liziwe had come to appreciate her mother's dependence on her around the house, and she felt affirmed and appreciated by this. She felt the security provided by her mother's presence in her life, and she loved the fact that her mother would always be available to answer the difficult questions, such as where the money would come from to buy food. In turn, Nonzame loved her daughter's self-driven nature. She loved the fact that she was not lazy and something didn't have to be repeated several times before she could move. There was a sense of teamwork between the two of them.

Now she was dead, and Liziwe felt the void, even as she lacked the ability to express it. Again, she shook her head, trying to pay attention to the task of sorting out the personal effects of her parents. In the room, there was a pile of neatly packed blankets, all stacked against the wall. Next to the blankets, she noticed an old and battered brown suitcase. It had been there for a while, but she had never particularly taken any notice of it. It was her mothers. Next to it was a blue painted metal case, which she called 'the trunk'. It was her father's. On top of the trunk there was a brown leather bag. This too was her father's. She thought about opening all the bags to see what was inside each of them, but soon resisted the temptation, figuring that she would do that when she had more time. Right now she needed to attend to Ntando and Tembisa who were finishing their breakfast in the middle hut. And so she left the room, fully intent on coming back to see what was in the bags.

But as she was walking slowly to the middle hut, still trying to make sense of everything that had happened, she saw Manyawuza coming, and stopped to greet her. Manyawuza was of course as always a daily visitor to the house. In fact in the mood Liziwe was in, she subconsciously wished to see Manyawuza, and to have somebody else to talk to.

"Hello Liziwe", said Manyawuza, again with unmistakable feeling in her voice, "did you guys sleep okay?"

Liziwe replied, "Oh yes Mam'Nyawuza we did, thank you."

"And did you eat anything today?" Manyawuza asked, and Liziwe again replied, "Yes mama, we cooked porridge, and there's still bread in the house."

"Well", said Manyawuza, "in that case, we have to wash the rest of the laundry, including the blankets. So if you don't mind I'll just be in the small hut."

Liziwe replied, "Okay mama, I'll probably join you later."

THESE ARE MY MOTHER'S CHILDREN

There were no streets in the village of Mcuncuzo, just walkways and footpaths. But the path past the Ncadana household was almost the main thoroughfare leading to the maize fields at the outskirts of the village, as well as to the McFarlane trading store about five kilometres away, which the locals called '*KwaMafelana*'. This McFarlane Trading store was the closest thing the villages had to a central business district. With the exception of state transactions, such as the payment of taxes, you could buy just about anything at this store - and it also served as a post office and a telephone exchange station.

On any day during the week, but especially on Mondays and on pension pay-out days, there would always be many people passing past the Ncadana household, headed to McFarlane's. Today there was double the traffic, as most of the people were also headed to the fields, bringing refreshments to the people ploughing the fields with spans of oxen. The whole village was alive with chatter and banter. Some people would stop momentarily at the house of Ncadana to enquire about the wellbeing of the children, and Manyawuza had become by default the main person to whom these enquiries were directed.

In fact, Manyawuza was about to enter the small hut after her brief chat with Liziwe, when she heard the voice of MamNgwevu, calling and greeting her enthusiastically. "*Nyawuza*! How are you today? Yho you're so scarce my friend. It's really been a while!" said MamNgwevu.

Manyawuza momentarily stopped what she was doing and walked over to the fence where MamNgwevu was standing, and replied, "Yho I'm fine Ngwevukazi, I'm just trying to tidy up here. Some of the work here is too much for the children to do alone."

MamNgwevu was also one of Nonzame's friends and neighbours, albeit her house was further away than Manyawuza's. She too was a well-known visitor to the Ncadana house, although not as frequent as Manyawuza. Today she was passing by, enroute to McFarlane's trading store.

Looking at Manyawuza, with concern in her voice, MamNgwevu asked, "How are they coping, the children I mean?"

"Well", replied Manyawuza, "as well as could be expected under the circumstances, I guess. I'm worried about the little one I must say."

MamNgwevu retorted, her face again a picture of concern, "Who, Ntando? Poor thing! I wonder if anything can be done. Children cannot just sit all by themselves without parents, surely."

"Indeed" Manyawuza replied, further saying, "But I must say Liziwe is strong, although in the end she too is a child."

MamNgwevu then said, trying to steer the conversation, "But I heard AmaQwathi had a meeting yesterday to discuss what is to be done about the house and the children."

Manyawuza replied, "Oh yes there was a meeting, and from what I heard, they want to close this house."

MamNgwevu, with her mouth now agape, said, "Close this house! And what about the children?!"

To which Manyawuza replied, with understated alacrity, "Hey *wethu*, they say the old one is now old enough to go and start her own house somewhere!"

Again MamNgwevu retorted, with shock, "Meaning what? That she must be married off?!"

"Exactly", Manyawuza said, and continued, "The way they see it is that, only in her own house, supported by her own husband, will she then be able to take proper care of her siblings, Tembisa and Ntando."

Clapping her hands in bewilderment, MamNgwevu said, "Amen! Now that is a horrible idea! When is this marriage supposed to take place?! And who's the suitor?"

Manyawuza replied, "I understand they have already identified Manyano's son, Dingalethu as the prospective husband."

Again clapping her hands, MamNgwevu said, "Oh my God! That old, ugly man?! Why would they want to do this to Nonzame's child?!"

Shrugging her shoulders in resignation, Manyawuza replied, "Beats me my friend! But I think part of it has to do with the fact that Nonzame has no one. As far I know, she has no surviving relatives. Her home in Mawusheni has been closed for at least the last five years. All her parents and siblings are late."

But MamNgwevu prodded on, "Does that mean this Dingalethu will take over this house?!"

To which Manyawuza replied, "Further down the line, yes I think that's the plan."

MamNgwevu, now totally besides herself with shock, asked, "And the children's education?!"

Manyawuza replied, sarcastically, "What 'children's education'? I don't think that's their priority. Even young Tembisa will be married off as soon as she reaches the same age as her sister now. And Ntando will become nothing more than everybody's herd boy."

"*Tyhini mntan' omNgwevu*! I don't believe this!" said MamNgwevu moving away from the fence, and continued, "Let me leave you *tshomi*, I still have to walk all that way to the trading store."

"*Kulungile wethu* Ngwevukazi" said Manyawuza, "I'm sure it's going to turn out alright in the end."

She waved to MamNgwevu and then proceeded to the small hut, to sort out the long ignored laundry, still talking to herself as if the conversation with MamNgwevu had not yet ended. What she did not know though was that as she was busy gossiping with MamNgwevu all this time, Liziwe had come into the small hut, initially with the intention of helping with the washing. She heard everything the two of them were talking about!

Manyawuza was shocked. She froze at the door, her mind racing, with questions abound. 'Did she hear us?' 'What did she hear?' 'What was she going to do now?' 'My God!'

As if reading and hearing Manyawuza's thoughts, Liziwe looked straight at her eyes, and said, "Yes mam' Nyawuza, I heard everything."

There was silence, and Manyawuza looked at Liziwe, her tiny frame suddenly looking big, like a tigress about to pounce. There was fire in her eyes, Manyawuza wryly observed. Looking at Manyawuza with unblinking eyes, Liziwe then said, very slowly and determinedly, with her hands interchangeably pointing in the general direction of the middle hut where Tembisa and Ntando were, and gesturing wildly,

> *"These are my mother's children, and this here is their home. They are not for sale. Nothing, and no one will lay a hand on them! And another thing, I am not going to go away and be a spouse to some man! If my relatives think they can parcel us off like that, I'm telling you, they have something else coming! Hell will freeze over!"*

Since the death of her parents, Liziwe had barely given a thought to what was going to happen to her, to Tembisa and to Ntando. She had been completely occupied with the immediacy of the events. But overhearing the conversation between Manyawuza and MamNgwevu had now jolted her to the reality of the situation.

Suddenly she became engrossed in thought, momentarily forgetting about Manyawuza, who in fact was standing at the doorway of the small hut, dumbfounded. Liziwe's mind was racing. She had questions, a string of them: How could these people do this? How could they even think of marrying her off to an ugly, smelly grown man? And how could they be so cruel to her sister and to her brother? Again, she swore to herself, that all this would happen only over her dead body!

With her eyes darting like an entrapped wild animal, she again looked at Manyawuza, and started to cry. She didn't make any crying sound. Tears just started to flow from both of her eyes, and without any attempt to wipe them off, she said, "So, what now?"

Manyawuza looked at her for a while without responding to the question. There was something different about Liziwe right now, Manyawuza observed. Suddenly she looked older and unlike a child, and she looked like someone not to be trifled with - a dangerous person.

But Manyawuza quietly chided herself for feeling intimated by a child, even though she of course felt acutely embarrassed. Seeing Liziwe standing there, next to the small hut's window, and listening to her conversation with MamNgwevu, had shocked her to the core. 'My God! I wish this child didn't hear this!' She kept muttering under her breath. She had not intended for Liziwe to know what AmaQwathi had discussed about her and her future. She was wary of being accused of gossip mongering and of butting into what was the business of AmaQwathi. As far as she was concerned, she was just a neighbour to the Ncadanas and it was not her place to communicate with Liziwe and her siblings the decisions of AmaQwathi. She was angry at herself for not taking precaution before talking to MamNgwevu.

Liziwe also compounded Manyawuza's predicament by her tone of voice and aggressive demeanour. It was the second time in as many days that Liziwe's audacity had shocked her. Manyawuza did not know what to make of this. Perhaps the child is under severe strain, with the death of her parents and everything else. But did she have a plan? What was she going to do if AmaQwathi went ahead with their plans? Manyawuza asked herself, getting none the wiser.

But Manyawuza was also concerned about her own reaction to being found out by Liziwe when gossiping with MamNgwevu. She had tried to say something, anything. But in spite of herself, she found that she couldn't. She was completely at a loss for words, and that scared her. Not wanting Liziwe to know was one thing, but being intimidated by her, as she was at that point, was something else entirely. What was that? But how could she have known the child was listening? And so what if she overheard the conversation with MamNgwevu anyway? She asked herself with a certain air of desperation. It's not as if she was never going to know ultimately, Manyawuza thought. Sure Liziwe was angry. Who wouldn't be at the prospect of being married off to some man you barely knew or cared nothing about? Still, she reasoned with herself, Liziwe is a child, a little girl. What could she do but accept her fate? As she asked these questions, she felt herself calming down and regaining her wits and composure.

At long last she responded to Liziwe's question, "I don't know my child. Whatever it is, we have to pray for the strength to overcome it." Without saying anything further, Manyawuza reached out to Liziwe, took her hand and said, "My child, repeat after me:

> *"The Lord is my shepherd; I shall not want. He maketh me to lie down in green pastures: he leadeth me beside the still waters. He restoreth my soul: he leadeth me in the paths of righteousness for his name's sake. Yea, though I walk through the valley*

*of the shadow of death, I will fear no evil: for thou
art with me; thy rod and thy staff they comfort me.
Thou preparest a table before me in the presence of
mine enemies: thou anointest my head with oil; my
cup runneth over. Surely goodness and mercy shall
follow me all the days of my life: and I will dwell in
the house of the Lord for ever. Amen."*

After this, Liziwe quickly checked on Tembisa and
Ntando. They were still finishing off their porridge, and
were taking their time about it, as Liziwe observed. But
she couldn't be bothered by this now. Her mind was still
occupied with what she just overheard from Manyawuza
and MamNgwevu. Looking at both Tembisa and Ntando,
without really speaking to them, Liziwe said, "I don't know.
I don't know what we're going to eat tomorrow, and I don't
know where all the money is going to come from. But I
know that I'd rather go blind than leave you guys alone and
go and marry some man!"

And then, just as Tembisa in particular was puzzling
over what Liziwe just said, Liziwe dashed out of the room,
and went again back to her parent's big hut. She was angry.
The conversation she just overheard between Manyawuza
and MamNgwevu had troubled her. How dare they?! She
seethed to herself. Without realizing it, she grabbed her
father's bag, and poured all its contents on the floor. Quite
why she did this, she could not say, nor for that matter, was
she aware of what she was looking for.

Liziwe pulled up her father's blue metal travelling case.
It was locked with a padlock and she didn't have the keys
for it. She pushed it back, figuring that perhaps, as she was

going through more of her father's things, she would find its keys.

There was also a brown leather bag. In it there were socks, underpants and pyjamas. In one of the side pockets there were the keys for the trunk padlock. This was a set of keys which included what looked like house keys, albeit, as Liziwe very well knew, not of this house.

Liziwe then opened her father's travelling case. She was not sure what she expected to find. All this was part of 'sorting out' things. Her father had not used any of his clothes since he arrived sick. He had been mostly in pyjamas.

As Liziwe opened the trunk lid, she could see that her father's clothes were all neatly folded. And as she opened the lid, she was met by a wafting smell of naphthalene. The trunk contained a range of clothing items – all reflecting the latest township fashion trends, which Liziwe knew absolutely nothing about, ranging from colourful bell bottom pants, heavy Brentwood pants, safari suits, Viyella shirts, shoes, including brands such as Crocket & Jones and Barker, etc.

At the bottom of the trunk there was a photo album, as well as a stack of letters, held together by a narrow rubber band. The album had a number of 'same time' Polaroid snaps, most of them showing her father posing against a green background, and sometimes posing with a telephone in the background, which clearly was part of a staged scenery.

In one or two of the photos, her father was standing alongside a strange and very beautiful woman. For a while Liziwe looked at the woman in the photo, wondering who she was. Even though she was wearing a domestic overcoat and her face covered with skin lightening cream, she was beautiful, with long Afro hair.

Liziwe's eyes wondered to the stack of letters. She looked at these letters, with surprise painted on her face. At the same time it was as if this was what she had been looking for. She turned the bundle around, and held it aloft against the sunlight, with her eyes squinting all the while. They all seemed to be written by a fountain pen, with the tell-tale smudges of ink in some of them. At her school they were using lead pencils in her class, but she had seen older pupils using these fountain pens, and always with ink-smudged shirt pockets.

As a Standard Five pupil, Liziwe could read, fairly well, and right now she was puzzled by this correspondence to say the least. She removed the rubber band, and spread the letters out on the floor. She counted them. There were seventeen letters, and all of them had the same beautiful handwriting.

Somehow she had expected that these would be from her mother. But they were not, and they were almost all expressing love and warm feelings, and all of them came from one Mavis. All of them were addressed to her father, Mandla Ncadana, to this address

McFarlane Trading Store
PO Box 47
Engcobo
5050

One letter read as follows:

> *114 Ontdekkers Road,*
> *Florida,*
> *Roodepoort*
> *1724*

> *My darling Mandla*

> *Oh how I miss you! This place is so cold without you. I swear one more day spent without you I'm gonna lose my head. I miss you desperately. If could, I would fly to where you are. But alas the circumstances won't allow. I shall wait for you then, till January when you come back. Lizeka said to say hi.*

> *Bye my love*

> *Mavis*

She picked up another letter. This was one of the oldest in the bundle, dated December 1977. In fact Liziwe noted that most of the letters were dated to coincide with the time when her father was at home for the December holidays. This one was brief, no more than a single paragraph, and it read:

> *114 Ontdekkers Road,*
> *Florida,*
> *Roodepoort*
> *1724*

> *Mr Darling Mandla*

> *My love I miss you so much! I hope you travelled home safely. I can't wait to see you again in January.*

Already it feels like it's been too long since you've been gone.

Yours in love

Mavis

Again, Liziwe picked up another letter – a more recent one, which in fact seemed to have arrived about three weeks ago. This was a bit sombre. It read:

114 Ontdekkers Road,
Florida,
Roodepoort
1724

Dear Mandla

I hope you are feeling better. Today I also finally managed to summon enough courage to go to the clinic. They say I'm positive!

PS: You left some of your stuff in my house. I'll put it all in the storage.

Mavis

Reading all these letters, Liziwe felt like she was intruding. The letters described a world that was totally foreign to her. It felt as though her father had been a complete stranger. She looked again at the letters, and wondered where her mother was in all this. Perhaps there's another stack of letters from her father to her mom, or the reverse, she wondered.

But more importantly, who was Mavis? What was she to her father? And who was Lizeka? She looked at the sender's address. She did not know any Mavis, and all these letters were indicating that she comes from number 114 Ontdekkers Road, Florida, Roodepoort. Liziwe had no idea where any of these places were.

Besides the letters, Liziwe noticed a big brown envelope, and inside it there was a large stack R10 bills. Liziwe had never seen this much money in her life! Of course in reality it wasn't that much money – certainly nothing more than a thousand rands.

Shocked, she pulled the trunk lid shut, and locked it. She then pulled her mother's bag closer and opened it. There was nothing in it, except for 'town clothes', which was to say these were the clothes her mother wore whenever she was going away. At the bottom of the bag were a set of papers tied together by a white twine. On closer scrutiny, Liziwe could see that these were clinic cards for all herself, Tembisa and Ntando. All their visits to the clinic, dates, consultation times, ailments, and medicine given, was meticulously recorded in these cards. Liziwe also established that the bag contained all their school reports from previous years.

When Liziwe was done looking at the personal effects of her parents, she stepped outside of the big hut. Even though it was still mid-morning, the temperature had quickly risen to above 30 Celsius, and was still rising.

To put it mildly, Liziwe was totally confused. The anger she felt at overhearing the conversation between Manyawuza and MamNgwevu had subsided somewhat and had been replaced by a newfound curiosity. She had questions - lots of them. Who was Mavis? What was she to her father? Did her mother know about this Mavis? From the letters it seemed that her father had another life entirely different from that which he had with his family at Mcuncuzo. Why? Of course her confusion was compounded by the fact that there was no one at that point who could answer her.

THE SILLY MEETING

It was just after ten o'clock in the morning when Liziwe finally emerged from her parents' big hut. By now the mercury had risen and the full glare of the summer sun was felt everywhere. With her head still buzzing with a string of questions, especially about her father's letters and the mysterious Mavis, Liziwe walked slowly from the big hut to join Ntando and Tembisa. As soon as they were again together in the middle hut, Tembisa, recalling what Liziwe had said just a few moments ago about being 'married off', asked teasingly, "So Liz, this man you're planning to marry, has he paid *lobolo* yet?" There was a twinkle in Tembisa's eyes as she asked her sister this.

Liziwe looked growlingly at her, at the same time asking herself, 'what did she know about lobola?!' She was well aware of Tembisa's rather slight but cutting humor. When she gets into a teasing mood you'd swear she's not only seven years old. One of the games they often played as children was called '*masithukathukane*', which Liziwe had long ago conceded. This was a game where each person would insult and mock the other, and whoever was the first to run out of things to say, or loses their temper, would be deemed a loser. Tembisa would always win this game hands down.

But just this at moment, Liziwe was not in the mood for games, even though she quite appreciated to see Tembisa's humor back. She looked straight at Tembisa and said, "Tembisa, *andidlal' ubonanje*! I'm not joking!"

Right at that moment, just as she was trying to intimidate Tembisa not to make fun of her, she saw the old men of AmaQwathi walking through the gate. There was going to be a meeting. She had not known about this, and in reality she could not have known what the elders of the family were planning. But having overheard from Manyawuza what their intentions were, Liziwe was now on tenterhooks.

As she looked at the men filing past her towards the front of the kraal, she was like a trapped cat. She counted about thirty elderly men going past her and taking their places near the kraal. And then she saw the man touted as her suitor. She felt a boiling rage inside. Not in this life! She seethed to herself.

As Dingalethu Mahomba and a delegation of AmaQithi were being directed to wait in the small hut, Liziwe was looking at him. It was the kind of loathing look normally seen when a person is looking at a cockroach.

To Liziwe, this Dingalethu, was a monster incarnate! He was just reprehensibly ugly, with no redeeming features. There he was, wearing old and torn blue overalls, worn out black mine boots with a steel tipped nose – the type called by labour immigrants '*amareeva*'. His head was covered with an out-of-colour black balaclava. He had a big belly, and his face was unshaven, looking like he had just woken up – even with dry drool marking both ends of his mouth, making him to look like he was wearing horse harnesses!

At about eleven o'clock in the morning, the meeting started. Manyawuza decided to stay with Liziwe and the children in the middle hut, which was a discreet distance away from the kraal, yet within earshot. She and Liziwe could hear as the leading men of AmaQwathi were talking. In fact Manyawuza was keenly looking forward to seeing how Liziwe would react to what the meeting was about to discuss - now that she knew what her relatives intended about her.

Looking at Liziwe restlessly pacing up and down, with her face wearing a frown, Manyawuza became even more concerned. She had the mind to walk over to old man Madevu and ask him to call off the meeting. But alas, she couldn't. It was too late, and more importantly, it was not her business.

As everybody settled to positions around the kraal, some sitting on boulders and bricks, and others on logs as well as on the grass, old man Madevu stood up to open the meeting, and said:

> *"My brothers, I have called you here so that we may conclude a discussion we already started last week. I therefore don't have to tell you why we are here. Needless to say, we are still in mourning. The passing of Mandla and his wife Nonzame is still raw in our hearts.*
>
> *I'm certain too that you all feel for Mandla's children, and as fellow AmaQwathi you have their interests at heart. These children cannot stay alone any longer than they already have. If we allow that situation to persist without arresting it, we will be opening space for the devil to play, and to take Mandla's children away from us.*

Today we must take a decision about who among us must take responsibility to look after this house, and we must take a final decision about what must happen to the children. I ask that you give these matters the benefit of your wisdom. Thank you."

As Madevu was sitting down, with his pipe in his mouth and frisking himself looking for a match, another man stood up. This was Nkosini, also a veteran of the clan of AmaQwathi, albeit it a few years younger than Madevu. His input was brief and to the point, and he said:

"MaQwathi! You have all heard what my brother just said. Indeed his word is true. If the children of Ncadana are left alone at this young age, they will not survive. Let us then confirm the decision we took last week - that the eldest daughter of Mandla and Nonzame will assume responsibilities as the wife of AmaQithi, who are here waiting in the small hut, ready to give effect to this.

We had also agreed that my sister, Mamanci will take care of the younger daughter, bring her up until she reaches the age of marriage.

We also agreed that my brother, Madevu, will take care of the boy and help him to become a man. Until then, this house shall remain closed. We shall of course appeal to the neighbours, especially Manyawuza and MamNgwevu, to keep an eye on it."

All other men that spoke after Nkosini repeated the same line - all of them expressing support for the manner in which AmaQwathi were going to safeguard the interests of the Ncadana children. When everybody had had their turn to speak, Madevu stood up again and said,

> *"That settles it then. I shall take the responsibility of talking to the children at a later stage. I do want to emphasize this point, that the decisions we have taken today are in the best interest of Mandla and Nonzame's children. I have no doubt that they too would have agreed under the circumstances, that this is the best manner in which their estate could be managed. This part of our meeting is concluded. We shall now, as AmaQwathi, put a question to these visitors from the house of AmaQithi. And that question is, why are they here today?"*

Madevu sat down as soon as he finished speaking. Even though it had been a short speech, he looked haggard and sombre. The latter part of his speech, which effectively was calling for the start of the lobola negotiations between AmaQwathi and AmaQithi, was intended to lighten the mood. Yet there was nothing jocular about his appearance, as if he would have preferred a different outcome to the meeting.

The delegation of AmaQithi which had come expressly for this part of the meeting, was asked to join everybody near the kraal. The question about why AmaQithi were there was not to be answered literally. It was an opening gambit to be responded to only by the offering a bottle of brandy. And what followed was the battering and banter that is associated with these kind of negotiations, which was to continue well into the night.

At this point, Liziwe, who, together with Manyawuza, had been listening discreetly from the middle hut, decided that she had heard enough! She walked out, leaving behind a bemused Manyawuza together with Tembisa and Ntando, who were playing among themselves and not paying attention to the meeting outside.

She walked around to the back of the hut, and with her arms akimbo, she looked into the distance, not for anything in particular. There was a bit of a fresh breezy air about which provided a welcome relief from the heat. As she stood there alone, feeling the soothing wind, she knew it. As soon as she heard AmaQwathi agreeing among themselves that she would be besotted to Dingalethu in a matter of a few days, and what she thought was the pejorative manner in which they discussed Ntando's and Tembisa's futures, she knew that this place was no longer her home. She took the decision at that point, that she and her siblings would leave - tonight!

She looked again into the distance, only this time suddenly noticing the undulating hills in her view, and wondering what lay beyond. Whatever that beyond portended, it was better than the impending reality of a forced marriage. "This is not going to happen!" She fumed to herself. "*Yhu! Khawufan' ucinge! Yini le*! Can you imagine me being a wife?! This is not happening!!" Tonight, she was going to leave her home, and the only thing that would change that is a demonstrable change of heart from her relatives.

She had no clear plan, nor any idea of what her destination would be. But she was resolute, that she would not stay at home any longer than was necessary. The little matter of where she would go, and how - she would think about those details on the way. Of immediate importance was to be as far away from this ghastly place as possible, and in double quick time. She thought of her father's duffel bag. She would pour all its contents into the metal case, so that she can use it for the journey. She would also take the stack of letters, the school reports her mother had kept, as well as the envelope with money.

With her mind definitely made up, Liziwe came back into the hut. She found Tembisa and Ntando were eating bread, downing it with Oro Crush drink. They were alone. Manyawuza had decided to also join the festive meeting near the kraal.

Liziwe looked at her siblings and rolled her eyes. On another day this would be funny. Tembisa did not know how to cut bread. She always made very thick slices which were tough to bite. Today she had plastered them with a thick layer of apricot jam, and both she and Ntando were literally rubbing their faces with jam and messing their clothes with it.

But Liziwe decided to ignore this, and before she knew it, she was crying. "Aw Liz, what is wrong now?!" Tembisa asked with a look of concern even as her face was covered in jam.

"We cannot stay here Tee. We need to leave, now!" Liziwe said. She did not wait for Tembisa's response or reaction. Instead, she dashed for the door.

"But Liz wait! Where are you going to now?!" Tembisa asked, with her voice now quivering.

Liziwe stopped momentarily and said, "I'm going to the big hut. We're going to need dad's bag."

Liziwe continued, looking at Tembisa, and all she could see was confusion and pleading eyes. She tried to compose herself, and slowly said:

> *"Tee, those grownups gathered out there want us to be married off to the old men of this village! For me they've chosen tat'uDingalethu as my husband, and for you they will still decide! In a few days I shall be a wife, and you shall be staying with granny Mamanci, waiting for your own husband, and Ntando will be staying with tat'uMadevu, waiting to be a man! We can sit here and allow all this to happen, or we can run away. For now I choose to run away."*

Tembisa and Ntando kept quiet. They did not understand what was going on, and could not comprehend what Liziwe had just said. But they could see that Liziwe was worked up about it. In fact, more than anything, Liziwe's demeanour kept them in check, as if afraid not to provoke her and cause more trouble. They watched as Liziwe brought their father's bag from the big hut and started to stuff it with their clothes.

SECTION THREE

THE WALK TO FATE

With Tembisa and Ntando looking on with even more curiosity, Liziwe stuffed all their clothes in her father's duffel bag, so quickly that in fact the packing did not last longer than twenty to thirty minutes. All the clothes were packed in, including school uniforms. By now it was about three o'clock in the afternoon. There was still a few more hours to kill before it would be dark. There was nothing much to do but while away time listening to the murmur of the meeting outside. The weather was good and the temperatures had by now dropped from the high of over 40 degrees Celsius to a cool 20°C.

As they were waiting, Tembisa, who still needed to clear her own confusion about this whole idea of running away, asked, "Liz, where exactly did you say we are going to?"

Liziwe replied curtly, "For now, we will go to Cofimvaba. We will decide things there."

"But", Tembisa pushed, "do you even know where Cofimvaba is?!"

"I do too!" Liziwe shot back. "The bus to Cofimvaba comes from the direction of Ncorha and goes over the hill there. If we follow the road, we shall not be lost!" Liziwe said, almost boisterously.

Tembisa shook her head, not out of disagreement, but in disbelief and wonderment, especially at the prospect of walking over that hill to Cofimvaba! But she accepted what Liziwe was saying, and she too had the same notion about where Cofimvaba was.

At just after eight in the evening, Liziwe gave the house one more look, refusing to think about whether or not she would miss it. She went to the big hut and locked the door with a small Vita padlock. She then went to the small hut, and again pulled the door and padlocked it.

As she passed past near the kraal, she could see and hear that the gathering of AmaQwathi and AmaQithi was still going on, albeit now completely inebriated. She could see some of the people looking at her with knowing looks. She looked down and pretended notice to notice the looks and whispers. Although there had been no home brewed beer prepared for this meeting, mainly because there couldn't have been so soon after a funeral, the delegation of AmaQithi had come bearing gifts – and these were now flowing freely.

Noting that besides the gossipy looks, none of the people gathered near the kraal were paying any particular attention to what the children were doing, Liziwe called Tembisa and Ntando together and said,

> *"Tee, we're going now. Just pull this door half ajar. We're not going to lock it, and we will leave the lights on. That way they will think we are still here. Just make sure there's nothing near the lamp that can catch fire should the lamp fall or something. Mam'Nyawuza will close the door when she comes in the morning."*

Liziwe then looked at Ntando. He was warmly dressed, with socks and shoes, a jersey and a beany hat, and she asked him, "Ntandos are you OK?" Ntando nodded his head and grabbed Tembisa's hand. This whole idea of 'going away' had somehow become an adventure he was now keenly looking forward to, as he said, "*Mna ndifun' uhamba mna!*" Liziwe then said, sounding like she was issuing a military command, "Let's go!"

With that, they were off. One by one, in single line formation, with Liziwe closely behind, the Ncadana children left their home under cover of darkness to a future and fate only God knew what it was. They walked, all along the gravel road that stretches from Qhumanco to Cofimvaba, first slowly, if not reluctantly with Liziwe and Tembisa taking turns in carrying Ntando on their backs.

If they were scared they never showed it. But, as it was, Tembisa was in fact scared. She had never been outside the yard of her home after dark. She had heard the scary stories told by her mother around the fireside - all fables with ghosts, witches and monsters that come at night. As they left their three rondavel house, Tembisa held on to Liziwe with one hand, while holding Ntando with the other, her own fear kept in check by Liziwe's determined steps and fearless demeanour. Still, as they cautiously made their way slowly away from their home, Tembisa nervously asked, "Liz, are you not scared? It's too dark."

As she asked this, in the distance they could see flashing lights. These were in fact the winged beetles, known as the lightening bugs, using their cold light to attract mates. But to the children they looked like an army of ghosts! Seeing this, Liziwe replied to Tembisa's question, "Well, I guess today we shall finally find out what it is that ghosts do. Whatever the case maybe, Tee, we cannot go back now!"

Liziwe was in fact also usually afraid of the dark, and Tembisa knew this. There was no electricity at Mcuncuzo and the only lights at night were from the moon and the stars, and on the days when those were not there, it was always pitch dark at night. Liziwe knew all about the fireside stories about ghosts, zombies, witches flying with brooms and riding bread, and because of all these things, she too never ventured outside the house at night.

But today, all throughout the journey, she would not even once seem concerned or fearful of the dark. The anger she felt at being given away would not allow her to give way to fear. Instead it served as the motivation to press on, and even more importantly, it gave Tembisa and Ntando the necessary assurance. For his part, Ntando was quiet, just sucking his left thumb and holding Tembisa's hand. He too was scared at first, but he quickly adjusted. He seemed resigned to accept whatever scheme his sisters had cooked up.

For a while the children walked in silence, all their senses tuned to every rustling sound. But for the most part all they could hear were the sounds of their own feet as they trundled the road. And then, out of the blue Tembisa broke into a song. It was a choral concert ditty she'd heard senior pupils at their school singing, which went like:

> *"Oh Lizzy Lizzy, Lizzy,*
> *Umhle wena, wena.*
> *Bonk' abantu,*
> *'Bantu bakhala ngawe,*
> *Wen' ungowam"*

It was odd, and so unexpected, but it seemed to lift their spirits up. Liziwe started to laugh, and then she joined the song, mimicking a bass male voice:

> *"Lizzy Lizzy mntakamama*
> *Umhle wena njengelanga*
> *Bonk' abantu bakhala ngawe*
> *Wen' ungowam"*

They all laughed at this, especially at Liziwe's very poor attempt at singing bass. But soon they became silent again, especially as Liziwe increased the walking pace. She was determined to quickly put as much distance between them and the village as was possible. At this stage her crude plan was to take the footpath from her home that joins the gravel road coming from the Ncorha direction, which in fact starts from Qhumanco further down.

The distance between the village of Mcuncuzo and the town of Cofimvaba is about fifteen kilometres. By car it feels a lot shorter, because even though it is a bumpy gravel road, it is fairly well maintained. But by feet it was all eternity.

THE BECKONING CITY LIGHTS

"We're almost there guys, we're almost there!" Liziwe said excitedly as she saw the city lights of the town of Cofimvaba emerging from the distance. It was about one o'clock in the morning. With tired legs and jarred nerves, but with their spirits still undaunted, the flickering city lights brought some relief among the children. Cofimvaba is of course a very small town, with nothing much in the way of neon lights. But what little light there was, was enough to generate immense excitement for Liziwe and her siblings.

Of course it took another thirty minutes before they could actually reach the town. At about half past one in the morning, they cautiously made their way towards the centre of town. There they were, walking slowly, carefully, their heads turning this way and that way - in the dead of night, alone and with no defined purpose for being there. For the first time, Liziwe started to feel afraid. It helped that Ntando was asleep at her back. But she could feel the tension in Tembisa as she tightened her grip on her hand.

The town was deserted, and spooky, as they moved towards the Roman Catholic Church building, probably attracted by its imposing facade. As they moved closer to the building, they saw a man standing near the gate. It was the security guard of the church, Matshaya, a fifty something year old man wearing a long overcoat and a dark beany hat. He had been standing in the shadows of the church's building when he saw the children coming a distance away. 'Now there's a curious sight!' he thought as moved out of the shadows and closer to the gate for a clear view. Of course he was used to seeing people walk into the church in distress. But he had never seen unaccompanied children coming into the church, much less at this hour.

With one look at the children he could see that there was a problem. They looked scared and also very tired, and even though they were near the church's gate, Matshaya could see that this was not really their destination. He opened the gate, as if enticing them to come in. Quite why he did this he could not be sure.

"What are you children doing here?" Matshaya asked, trying to make his voice not as gruffly is it probably sounded. Before anyone of them could answer, Matshaya again shot with another string of questions, "Where are you going to? Who are you? My God! Do you know how dangerous it is for children to walk alone in town at night?!" He asked these questions without actually waiting for answers.

Liziwe froze. She held Tembisa back - and just stared at the man like an animal in a fight or flight mode. The security guard, sensing that the next reaction from these children was probably either to scream or run away, said, 'Come in, come in my children. You look cold. I have fire here.'

Liziwe stood still for a while longer. Matshaya could hear her thinking, and weighing her options. And then slowly and reluctantly, she moved towards the gate which Matshaya was holding slightly open, and nervously went inside the church grounds, all the while her eyes firmly trained on Matshaya.

Matshaya closed the church gate and directed the children to a room at the back of the church. This was a room used by parishioners, especially when they had to sleep overnight when church events ran longer than normal mass time. Inside the room there was a large stack of foam mattresses. Matshaya pointed Liziwe to these mattresses, and said, "There, you can pull one of those, and sleep. I'll bring you something to eat."

As he dashed out to organize food, Tembisa threw herself onto the mattresses, saying, "Liz, *ndiyozela mna*, I want to sleep! I don't care about the food." Liziwe didn't reply to this, she just gestured for her to go right ahead. She was still very suspicious, and she kept saying to herself, 'this Matshaya, *ndimjongile*. He had better not be planning anything!'

Matshaya returned later with a brown loaf of bakery bread and fizzy drinks. But already Tembisa and Ntando were asleep on the mattresses, without blankets. It didn't matter anyway because it was warm. Only Liziwe was awake and still pacing up and down the room. Matshaya put the drinks and the bread on a small table in one corner of the room, and said, "So who are you my child?" Ordinarily Liziwe would look down when talking to a grown up, but in this instance she looked straight at Matshaya's eyes and said, "My name is Liziwe Ncadana. These are my siblings."

Matshaya looked at the children as they slept, like they have been asleep for a long time, and said, "Is there anything wrong, at home maybe?"

Liziwe replied, "Well nothing, and something... It's a long story."

"It usually is my child, it usually is", said Matshaya with a look of concern, and then continued, "Where are you going to?"

"Well", said Liziwe, again maintaining eye contact with Matshaya, "We are hoping to catch a taxi or bus or whatever, to Roodepoort." On hearing herself saying this out loud, she shook her head slightly, as if in dispute with her own thoughts. Up to this point, she had not actually thought about her plan beyond arriving in Cofimvaba.

Matshaya made a whistling sound, shaking his head in amazement. He had worked in the mines for most of his youth, and momentarily he found it strange that Liziwe would specifically make mention of Roodepoort, which she pronounced as 'Rudepot'. As far as he knew, most people who go to the Transvaal part of the country would just say they are going to 'Johannesburg' or 'Egoli' or 'Rhawutini'. Matshaya put this to a possibility that this was where the children's parents were, and that they were now enroute to them. Quite why they were walking into Cofimvaba at this ungodly hour, he put it to the crazy things children do these days! Whatever the real story was, it was not his business. He would report this incident to the Reverend first thing in the morning, and be done with it, he thought.

Matshaya gave Liziwe one more look, and then said was, "Well my child, there's food. When you are done you can then pull a mattress and sleep. My shift ends at six, but if you need to know where taxis and busses are, I'm sure the Reverend will show you where they are. They all leave in the afternoon. Good night my child." Liziwe felt a strong sense of relief as she said, "*Enkosi tata*", and she closed the door. She too was not hungry. All she wanted to do was to sleep.

A PRAYER FOR THE ROAD

"*Nkqo nkqo*! May I come in?" Liziwe heard the voice of a man knocking at the door of the church room where she and her siblings were sleeping. It was about ten o'clock in the morning, and the knock on the door was literally waking them up. It was Father Dinga, the reverend at the Cofimvaba parish of the Roman Catholic Church. In all her life, Liziwe had never slept till this time of the day. She was a bit disoriented at first, but soon regained her senses.

Waking up this late, in a strange place, Liziwe panicked at first, thinking that they had overslept and were late. She looked around frantically for Tembisa and Ntando, but soon relaxed a little bit when she saw that they were still asleep next to her. But as she was roughing Tembisa and Ntando to wake up, Father Dinga stopped her, saying, "Relax my child, it's only ten o'clock. Matshaya did tell me that you will be catching a taxi to Jozi." Liziwe interjected, "A taxi to where?! And who are you?" She had never heard of this place before and it was not where she was going to! She also recalled that Matshaya had said something about a priest that would come in the morning.

Again Father Dinga gestured for her to relax, and said, "It doesn't matter my child. Don't worry so. You and your siblings are not late. I am Father Dinga. You can wake up now and wash. There is warm water. They will bring you food afterwards."

Liziwe looked at Father Dinga as he was speaking to her. He was tall and slightly built, wearing grey pants and a black shirt with a white collar. He looked like was in the process of getting ready to go someplace, and then it occurred to her that today was a Sunday.

About an hour later, the children were done washing and changing their clothes, and then they ate wheat porridge, followed by bread and Jabula soup. When they were done, Father Dinga came back into the room again and said,

> *"My children, before I accompany you to the taxi rank, let us pray:*
>
> *Father God, I bring to you these children. Yesterday they walked all night, and you guided them to your House. They walked in the dead of night, with beasts that could have harmed them, abound. Yet you offered them your protection and your comfort. Indeed Heavenly Father, we are, all of us, in a journey to somewhere - and ultimately to you. These children have begun theirs today. Wherever it is that they are going to, my Lord, whatever it is that torments and troubles their young souls, be with them to the end of their journey. Amen"*

When Father Dinga was done with the prayer, everybody stood up. Liziwe picked up the duffel bag that their clothes, and asked Tembisa to hold Ntando's hand. With Father Dinga leading the way, they were off to the taxi rank, which was about 150 meters away from the church.

When they arrived, Father Dinga extended his hand to Liziwe and said, "Well my child, here are the taxis. You are the first ones to arrive, so it's gonna be a while before you can be on your way. Once again good luck and God bless."

Liziwe replied, "Thank you Father, thank you indeed for everything. I don't know what we would have done without you. Thank you very much, and please express our appreciation to tat'uMatshaya as well." Father Dinga, turning to walk away, said, "Will do my child, good bye."

As Father Dinga was quickly making his way back into the church, leaving Liziwe and her siblings at the taxi rank, Liziwe looked around at the taxis more closely. She saw the fleet of taxis, all standing in a row. There were people moving up and down, literally yelling their various destinations.

She turned to Tembisa, who at this time was carrying the duffel bag with their clothes, and said, "Tee, wait. Give me the bag. Let me get the envelope with money. I also need one of the letters from daddy's stack."

Tembisa handed the bag over without saying anything and almost in an absent minded fashion. All she cared about at that point was to get inside these taxis and feel them drive, and she could not be bothered by why her sister wanted money or letters.

The taxi rank was full with taxis of all kinds of makes and colours. Liziwe did not know anything about cars, how they were made and by whom. But she did notice that predominantly there was a number of Toyota Hi Ace Super 10s as well as VW Microbus 2000ls.

She approached one of the taxis that was indicating its destination as Johannesburg. The driver of this taxi was a tall and chubby fellow wearing a leopard skin vest, green trousers, which in fact were part of a two piece overall, and sandals. In one hand he was holding a brown wooden clipboard, and on the other he was clutching a stack of money. As Liziwe approached, she could hear him shouting as he called for passengers, "Egol' Egol' Egoli!"

Liziwe walked up to him and said, "Hello Mister, I and these children here are going to this place". And she handed the driver the letter with Mavis's address. The driver looked at the letter, with eyes squinting, and then said, "I see. This is Roodepoort, right?"

Liziwe nodded her head. The driver then said, handing the letter back to her, "OK, but you'll be the last ones to get off. The fare for the three of you will be R400 – R150 for you, R150 for the young lady here, and R100 for the lad. Take the seat just behind the driver, so that you can get off quickly if you need to, seeing that you're all minors. Meanwhile, get my money ready. I'll take it just before we go."

The children needed no further invitation. They got into the taxi, fascinatedly looking at the big steering wheel and the dashboard controls. About two hours later the taxi filled up with other passengers. The driver came by one more time to check everyone against a passenger list, and collected all outstanding payments, and then got behind the wheel.

Sitting next to the window as the taxi was driving at a gentle pace, whizzing past villages and towns, Liziwe felt herself beginning to get morose again. It had been a topsy turvy period - from the death of parents, to her relatives resolving to marry her off. All her preoccupation in these last few days had been about looking after the children, and in all this time since they left home under cover of darkness, she had been thoroughly focused on getting away, and had not had any moment to doubt her course of action.

Yet as she sat in the taxi, staring through the window, her eyes unfocused and not really seeing anything, her tears were running down her cheek. For a brief moment, she wondered if anyone back home was looking for them, she began to have doubts, and started to wonder if the whole thing was a good idea. 'Where are we going to? Where am I taking my mother's children? What if something goes wrong?' She asked herself.

But then again she thought of home, and of Dingalethu! But besides the past, she was also worried about getting lost in Roodepoort, about who Mavis really was, what she would say or do to them when they arrive, and whether she would actually come back if things didn't go well. And then she heard her own voice, rasping 'Never!'

SECTION FOUR

SECTION FOUR

THE CHILDREN AT THE GATE

"Now who on earth could that be?!" Marike le Roux wondered out loud as she watched a beige Toyota Hiace minibus taxi, which had pulled up in front of her house. Marike's house, typical and unassuming, was hidden behind tall trees and neatly trimmed hedges. It was the corner house at number 114 Ontdekkers Drive in Florida, just outside the town of Roodepoort. You would not see this immediately when looking at it for the first time, because from the main street all you would see is a big mahogany door that seemed to blend with the trees around the house. But it was in fact a big and sprawling mansion, with a beautifully manicured lawn, a sparkling swimming pool, and with accommodation galore at the back for guests and servants.

The house belonged to Fred and Marike Le Roux, both of whom were currently pensioners. Fred had been a teacher for over thirty years, with teaching stints in provinces such as the Orange Free State, Natal and Transvaal - where her last teaching post was, at the nearby Florida Primary School. Marike on the other hand had been a nurse at clinics and hospitals all throughout the Transvaal for over twenty five years, with her last post being also at the nearby Flora Clinic.

Besides being public servants, Fred and Marike had also been accomplished commercial farmers prior to their retirement, and owned vast amounts of farming land in the Orange Free State. But as they grew older, they decided to settle in Roodepoort, and leased their farms. By every reckoning, they were a wealthy couple, albeit understated.

Today, being a Sunday, Marike was up very early in the morning to prepare to go church - the NG Kerk which was about two hundred metres from her house. But to her surprise, it was raining, and looking at it bucketing down, Marike just knew it that going to church today was out of the question. She and Fred were not religiously devout anyway even though they attended church regularly.

Besides, her right leg was feeling heavy. It was not painful as such. But it was as if it's not even there, and she needed the help of a walking stick to walk around the house. As she looked at the rain hitting her window panes hard, she decided she would not dare drag herself into this weather.

But her sudden decision not to go to church seemed to immobilize her somewhat. She had woken up with the express purpose of preparing for church. But now, sitting alone in the kitchen, she became pensive, and was torn between going back to bed and hanging around in the house looking for something to do. She was also vaguely troubled by the fact that Fred was still asleep in their bedroom.

Quite why Fred was still asleep at this time, she couldn't say. But it was unusual. She tried to put it out of her mind. Perhaps, she thought, it was the susurrating sound of the rain as it pounded the roof and the window panes that dulled him to more sleep. Or perhaps he was just tired after having slept late the previous night. Perhaps it had to do with their visit to Dr Hans Maree the previous day.

Thinking about Dr Hans Maree, Marike let out a heavy sigh. She had tried after their visit to Dr Maree to be cheerful and positive. But no matter how she looked at it, the news was not good, and she found that there was nothing she could say or do that could hide that. The doctor, the third is as many days, had confirmed their worst fears. As if that was not enough, not only did Dr Maree confirm that Fred had a malignant brain tumor, he also confirmed that Marike's diabetes was now officially out of control - that the nervous tissue in her right leg was now almost completely damaged.

They both knew, from previous consultations with doctors, that an amputation of her right leg was inevitable. And now, this confirmation of Fred's brain tumor provided the clearest indication yet, at least as far as Marike was concerned, that certainly there were troubles ahead – that these developments are life changing events. The onset of a terminal disease in their lives was something they both had dreaded, especially since they retired. It was one of the reasons they decided to leave their farm in the Orange Free State and be closer to clinics and hospitals.

Marike recalled the many discussions they had about not wanting to be a burden to society should it ever happen that they were no longer able to take care of one another. They had discussed and agreed on all scenarios, including ending it all as soon as there was confirmation of terminal illness afflicting either or both of them, long before such illness renders them into a vegetative state.

Whatever the reasons were about why Fred was still asleep this late in the day, being alone in the kitchen seemed to put Marike in a gloomy and morose mood. Trying to fight off this downcast mood, she decided to make herself a cup of coffee. Although she was not a heavy coffee drinker, her day did not begin without a strong simmering cup. Her mood was also not helped by the fact that, Mavis, her maid of over fifteen years, had taken a day off today. Normally, Mavis would make the coffee as and when she needed it, but especially in the morning.

Marike pulled a kitchen stool and sat down. Almost absent mindedly, she cast a panning look through the kitchen window into the distance. She could see the train traffic out of the Roodepoort train station, taking goods and passengers to and from Johannesburg and to areas such as Krugersdorp and Randfontein.

In the distance she could also see the smoky silhouette of the Dobsonville township. She had never been to Dobsonville in all the fifteen years Mavis worked and stayed at her house, she thought as she squinted her eyes for a better view. Yet she felt like she knew the place. For one thing, most of the support staff she had hired over the years, the maids and 'garden boys', all came from Dobsonville. They had houses there which they returned to at the end of the day, or every time they had a day off.

The thought made her uncomfortable. She started to fidget, and held the coffee mug tightly with both hands. Not sufficiently aware of the reasons she felt this way, but it suddenly it occurred to her that she did not know much about Mavis - not her surname, and definitely not her place of birth! She did not even know her address in Dobsonville. All she knew was that Mavis stayed somewhere at Mphephetho Drive in Dobsonville. Whenever she needed transport home, or she needed her to come to work on days when there was no public transport, she would drop or pick her up near the Dobsonville Police Station, which was on the outskirts of the township.

She stood up, with the support of her walking stick, still with her cup of coffee in hand, and limped slowly, feeling the pain in her leg with every step, over to the lounge, which was directly facing the front gate of the house. From here she could see the main road, and even this early in the morning, it was busy. On both sides of the road there was a bus stop, which was also visible from her lounge. Taxis, mainly from Johannesburg carrying passengers to places such as Roodepoort, Kagiso, near Krugersdorp, and Mohlakeng, near Randfontein, also used these bus stops for brief stopovers on both directions.

It was while she was beginning to settle in one of the settees in her lounge, still mildly curious about why Fred was still asleep, that Marike's attention was drawn momentarily to a beige taxi that pulled up on the bus stop directly opposite her house, from the Johannesburg direction.

The taxi was different from the usual lot. For one thing, it had unusual number plates, starting with the letters XD, unlike most traffic here which carried the TJ letters denoting Johannesburg. Seeing that she did not know the town represented by the number plates, she pulled the telephone, which was sitting on a small wooden stand next to the couch she was sitting on, and decided to call Captain Van Huyssteen of the Roodepoort Police to enquire about the meaning of these number plates. Captain Van Huyssteen promptly told her that the X part of the plates is reflecting the new independent homeland of the Transkei, and then hung up.

With all her curiosity levels now raised, Marike sat up straight and looked at this taxi. All her senses were now pricked. She observed that as soon as the taxi stopped, the driver got out to open the passenger door, after which three children alighted. She observed as the driver was gesturing in the direction of her house, as if showing the children where to go, and then as he got back into the taxi and drove off.

'Nee maan, wat gaan nou hier aan?! 'This is bizarre!' said Marike to herself, almost screaming as she observed the three little children standing and looking as if they're lost in front of her gate. She thought about going out to see what they wanted, but there was something about these children that held her back.

Looking at the oldest one, a girl, and for a minute she thought it was Lizeka, Mavis's daughter. But there was something odd about Lizeka today. Who were these children she was with? And why was she so scrawny and somewhat unkempt and dishevelled today? And why was she knocking at her door? Usually Lizeka knew her place. She knew not to bother the Mrs at the big house, and to use the side entrance to the servants' quarters.

At first Marike felt a tinge of irritation at this flagrant lack of respect. 'Mavis knows not to let her children into my house!' She fumed quietly to herself. But the irritation slowly yielded to mild curiosity – as it hit her. This was not Lizeka, but someone who seriously looked like her! Instinctively she decided to open the door. She had never allowed a black person through this door before, not even those who came to fix things in the house.

Of course Marike's curiosity was only matched by Liziwe's apprehension. For one thing, not only had she never seen a white person before in her life, but being this close to one compounded her fears. She listened to Mrs Le Roux as she was saying things like, "Come in, come in children! Who are you? What do you want?" Liziwe did not answer, even though she could hear her. It occurred to her that even though at her school back in Mcuncuzo they were taught English, she had never actually spoken it!

Seeing that she was not responding to her questions, Marike quickly assumed that maybe she couldn't understand English. And so she decided to try the mine workers' language, *fanakalo*, and said, "*Wena funa lo ntoni?*" To Liziwe this sounded like the most horrible way of speaking isiXhosa, and without thinking, she blurted out, "Mavis!"

"Do you know Mavis?" Marike asked, becoming more curious, and also quickly corrected herself, saying, "*Wena yazi lo* Mavis?"

Liziwe shot back, "No", again feeling acutely irritated by this strange "Xhosa" being spoken in this place!

"Does she know you?" Again Marike asked, and again the curt response from Liziwe was "No."

Marike realized that any answers she wanted to get out of this child, she would have to get them by some other means. To say that she was a combination of astounded and confused would be an understatement! Part of her wanted to show the children the door, but curiosity got the better of her. Liziwe's striking resemblance with Mavis's daughter Lizeka was just too much.

Without thinking, she called out for Fred, "Fred honey, will you wake up already?! Fred le Roux emerged from the bedroom looking dazed and disoriented, and walked into the kitchen, where Marike was. "What now?" He asked, looking accusingly at his wife. Clearly he didn't like his sleep to be interrupted in this way.

"These children are looking for Mavis", said Marike pointing Fred in the direction of the lounge where Liziwe and her siblings were sitting. "So, what's that got to do with me?" Fred shot back, frowning in puzzlement.

"Fred dear", said Marike with appealing eyes, "I think we have a situation here."

"Well dear", said Fred, interrupting his wife, "I'm all ears."

"Fred I'm serious", Marike said with a touch of impatience, "We have a situation here. I think these children are related to Mavis in some way. The resemblance between the older child and Mavis's daughter is too strong to be a coincidence. I don't know what the situation is, but it looks serious."

"Oh yeah, and what do you suggest we do about that honey bun?" Fred asked, now feigning more interest.

Marike replied, "Mavis is coming to work tomorrow. I suggest we open her room and allow these children to wait for her there."

"Well, whatever", said Fred, dismissively. 'How do you think Mavis is gonna take this – being surprised by children like this?" He asked.

"Let's see what happens tomorrow dear. In the meantime, make yourself a cup of coffee. I'll show the kids the room. They're probably dead tired and hungry." Marike said, as she beckoned for Liziwe, Tembisa and Ntando to follow her.

MEETING FATHER'S OTHER WOMAN

"Lord I wonder what awaits in this house of horrors!" Mavis said, talking to herself as she alighted from a taxi in front of the Le Roux house where she worked. She had no idea what lay in store for her. But her concern was not about anything else other than the amount of work that was waiting for her. She knew that Marike was not a good housekeeper. Every time when she'd been away on leave she'd find a stack of unwashed dishes in the kitchen sink, waiting for her, and all the rooms in the house would be in a mess, with beds unmade and clothes scattered on the floor.

She checked her wristwatch as she entered the house through the kitchen door as usual. It was exactly six o'clock in the morning. Her normal starting time at work was seven o'clock, but she had also established a practice of going on duty as soon as she arrives, something which always made her grumpy about her pay.

She found Marike standing next to the kitchen sink, sipping a cup of coffee. 'Oh my God, she's actually waiting for me, at this time!' Mavis noted wryly. "Good morning madam, I hope I'm not late", she said, wondering why

Marike would be waiting for her instead of being still in bed as she usually would be at this time.

Marike replied, "Morning Mavis, we have to talk." Mavis froze for a moment. 'We have to talk' was not good, she thought "What's wrong? Am I being fired madam?!" She asked looking suspicious. *"Ag nee maan, moenie so wees nie*! Nothing of the sort. But before you start your duties, I suggest you go to your room. You have guests. They arrived yesterday. Please don't worry about me and Fred." Marike said, and this latter point was deliberately made to prevent Mavis from hiding the children in her room as she normally does with her daughter Lizeka.

Confused, puzzled and curious, Mavis went to her room. 'In God's name, what guests would these be?' She wondered as she reached the door of her room. Slowly she opened the door, without knocking. And there they were. The children were all seated on the floor, and the room was clean, with no evidence that they had slept here. For a moment Mavis was taken aback. 'Children!' 'Are these the 'guests' the madam was talking about?' 'What in heaven's name is all this?'

And just as she was asking herself this string of questions, she saw Liziwe's face, and for a split second she thought it was Lizeka, her daughter. But even as she thought that, she knew it couldn't be. Lizeka was in Dobsonville, where she left her still sleeping. Besides, Lizeka was not slender like the child she was looking at right now. "What the hell?!" Mavis heard herself exclaiming out loud. "Who the hell are you?!" She asked.

Liziwe, who had been silently watching Mavis from the moment she stepped into the room, replied, with confidence "My name is Liziwe. This is my sister Tembisa, and my brother Ntando. I believe you know my father, Mandla Ncadana."

Mavis had tried before in her life to learn to whistle. Each time she would bite her tongue and her cheeks would get tired from having to blow air, and nothing would come out. But today she puckered up and heard herself whistling her shock!

"Mandla sent you here? To me?!" She asked, feeling the initial shock yielding to anger at this daring act by her ex-boyfriend. Liziwe replied coolly, and matter-of-factly, "No, he couldn't have. He's dead. Both he and my mother are dead."

Mavis looked at Liziwe blandly, and said, as she grabbed a chair, "Alright, you had better explain yourself." With astounding cogency and clarity, Liziwe proceeded to narrate the whole story that led to her and siblings being in Roodepoort at that moment. When she was done, she said, "There you are, that's our story."

Again Mavis shook her head in utter amazement. She had listened to Liziwe attentively, hanging onto almost every word coming out of her mouth. She looked at Liziwe again, up and down, trying to figure her out. She was struck by the fact that Liziwe had just told her a story of grief and misery – without seeming miserable.

Mavis stood up, as if feeling the weight of the whole world descending on her shoulders, and paced up and down the small room without saying anything, other than repeating the word, "Amazing!"

And then as if she had an afterthought, she asked, "Did you have anything to eat this morning?" To which Liziwe replied, "Yes, we found out where everything is, and the lady in the big house also helped us."

"I bet she did!" Mavis said, and then returning to the matter at hand, she continued, "So Liziwe, here we are. You and your siblings have taken this journey from Mcuncuzo to Egoli. Frankly I'm still amazed that you actually did this, tracing me up like this, and taking this very big risk. But you have not told me - what do you want? Why are you here?"

Liziwe didn't answer immediately. She didn't fidget or act as if she's searching for a way to answer. Instead she stood up, walked slowly, deliberately towards the room's only window and looked into the distance, and then said, "I want you to look after my mother's children."

She turned around, quickly enough to see Mavis's ashen faced look of horror, and before Mavis could say anything, Liziwe continued, looking straight into Mavis's eyes, "You are the closest thing these children have to a mother. If you loved my father as I've heard your heart proclaiming, then you'll love his children too."

Mavis was shocked, and bewildered. She felt like she was in a dream and a nightmare all at the same time. At one level she was angry. This child, how dare she! But she checked herself. There was a certain self-assuredness about Liziwe which she found both endearing and slightly intimidating at the same time. And she found it interesting that Liziwe didn't seem to include herself as part of the children that needed to be taken care of. After a while, Mavis managed to find her voice again, and asked, "If I do that - profess my love to your mother's children, as you say, what do you expect me to do about it?"

"Well, to answer your question as directly as you've put it", said Liziwe, "I want you to take us into your care. No doubt it's an imposition for which there may be no reward in the end. All I can promise is our gratitude."

Mavis again slowly shook her head, still astounded by the clarity of Liziwe's expression and her confident demeanour. After a long pause, Mavis then said, "I'm going for a walk. I need to think. In the meantime, make yourselves at home. I'll be back as soon as possible."

Mavis was still shaking her head in disbelief as she walked out of the room, leaving the children to watch TV. She walked along the Ontdekkers Road highway, towards the Florida Mall, which was about five hundred metres away. To say she was in a state would be an understatement. She didn't even hear the buzzing sound of traffic on the road, as her mind was on Liziwe, her unannounced visit, and definitely her unrealistic request, which sounded pretty much like an ultimatum of some sort!

All along the way Mavis kept talking to herself, saying things like, 'This Liziwe kid is something, is she not? *Tyhini Bawo*! Quite a feisty bloody minded risk taker, she is! *Nkosi yam*! What am I going to do with all this?'

About the news that Mandla was dead, Mavis was not shocked. She was aware that Mandla had been ill, and she had a good idea of the cause of it. But for Liziwe to hop on a taxi to Egoli to impose on a dead relationship was too much, Mavis thought. Feeling hot under the collar, she did not even notice that she was in fact talking to herself, saying:

> *'Surely this child is stretching the concept of love beyond reasonable bounds! By what right is she expecting me to take care of her and her siblings? I was a girlfriend to Mandla, not a polygamous wife. There is surely no sense in law, in tradition, or in common sense, where I could inherit the children of a marriage, now dissolved by death, in which I was*

the other woman! What then obligates me to look
after the children of a marriage I wasn't part of?'

Mavis got stuck on this latter part of her own question. She thought about the striking resemblance between Liziwe and Lizeka and again said aloud, 'I wasn't part of?!' She repeated the line, her thoughts trailing off, but ended up saying,

> *'But if I say no to this, what will become of these*
> *children? Doesn't the knowledge of their possible fate*
> *implicate me into action? More importantly, these*
> *are my daughter's relatives - sisters and brother. I*
> *can't knowingly send them to oblivion, can I?'*

Mavis sighed as she also reached the shopping centre, only to find that not only did she not know what she wanted to buy, she had even left her wallet back in the house. So she just turned around and walked the same distance back, only this time her steps were more purposeful.

When she finally arrived back to her servants' quarters at Marike's house, Mavis found the children playing around the room. They were laughing at something little Ntando had said, and they seemed to be absolutely oblivious to the world and its troubles – just happy and enjoying one another's company. Looking at the scene in front of her, Mavis decided to retreat to an adjacent room, which was empty, to pray:

> *"Father God, many a time I've knelt down on*
> *my knee, in front of you, asking, begging, and*
> *beseeching you for your blessings. Today I see these*

three little children, knocking at my door, asking, not for water or bread or shelter, but for me to be their parent. They travelled great distances, crossing many rivers and passing many towns, at the risk of loss of limb and life, to put this request to me. I am, as you know, a woman of no means. I have on several occasions brought my situation to your attention, seeking your divine intervention. Yet here I am today contending with a decision that may save the children and destroy me. But, as I know, and accept unconditionally the fact of your infinite wisdom, I know that these children are not, and cannot, be your way of punishing me for the sinful life I've led. I know that with these children you are affirming me, and you are giving me a responsibility, which I must unfailingly carry out. Consequently, I accept, and I pray for strength and your guidance. Amen."

Soon after finishing her prayer, and with her mind now made up, Mavis went back to the room where Liziwe and her siblings were playing. For a while she stood at the doorway, looking at the three children, and muttered wryly under her breath, "God has a weird sense of humour! Now suddenly I'm a mother to three grown up kids - without bothering about sex!"

As she stood there, watching the children, Liziwe and her siblings were fully engrossed with the small black and white Blaupunkt television. There was nothing on, just a round colourful pattern, but the kids were fascinated by it.

Mavis finally cleared her throat, and said,

"Look, I don't know what all this means. But for now you can stay - till I figure out what to do, that is. You will stay here with me for the rest of this week, till I'm off, and then you'll come with me to Dobsonville. In the meantime I want you to help me with cleaning the madam's house. You can't just sit here and do nothing hey."

Liziwe was visibly relieved. She had had horrible thoughts about all this going wrong, and the thought of going back home was just too much to bear. She looked at Mavis, with her eyes welling with tears, and said, "Thank you aunt Mavis, thank you indeed!" Mavis too could see the relief in Liziwe's whole demeanour. For the first time she looked like the child that she really was, even referring to Mavis respectfully as 'aunt Mavis'.

"Come, come now!" Mavis said tapping her gently on her shoulders, "We have work to do. I need to show you around the place, thereafter I'll have a talk with the madam. She seems to have taken a liking to you. Maybe I can also get her to allow Tembisa and Ntando to play in the yard till the end of the week. Come, let's all go to the big house."

A minute later, Mavis, with Liziwe, Tembisa and Ntando in tow, entered Marike's main house through the kitchen door. Marike was standing near the kitchen window, seemingly in deep thought. Mavis could hear the sound of running water, a sign that Fred was taking a shower. When she saw them coming in, Marike composed herself, and said, "Oh good, here you are!"

"Yes mam", said Mavis, thrusting Liziwe forward, and continued to say, "I don't know if you were properly introduced."

Marike interjected, saying, "I can't say that we have. But we did meet briefly."

"Well", said Mavis, pointing to each of the children, "This is Liziwe, this is Tembisa, and this is Ntando. I'll tell you all about their story when there's time. Suffice it to say, if you don't mind, they will stay with me for a week, and thereafter we will all move to my place in Dobsonville. I've also asked Liziwe to help me out with the work while she's here."

"That's ok my dear", said Marike cheerfully, "Let's talk later then. I'll be out of your way. This place is a mess. In the meantime I shall need your Reference Book. You can just put it on the coffee table when you can, I'll get it later." Marike said, and she stood up, looked at Liziwe again, with questioning eyes, and walked out.

Mavis was puzzled at why Marike would need her Reference Book. As she set about her work in the house she kept repeating this line to herself, 'Now she wants my Dompas!' But her mind went back to Liziwe yet again. With the initial shock of Liziwe's unannounced visit, and her astounding 'request' now beginning to fade, Mavis soon realized that the arrival of these children into her life had introduced a new crisis – that if she was going to keep Mandla's children, she would have to re-evaluate her own life and make adjustments.

With Tembisa and Ntando playing and running around in Marike's yard, and she and Liziwe working inside the house, Mavis found that she cannot concentrate. There were aspects of her life heavily impacted by today's events. What did this mean? Was she going to cope with five children in her maid's wages? And how was she going to explain this to Mxolisi? 'Oh my God, Mxolisi!' She exclaimed, as if suddenly remembering something she should not have forgotten in the first place. She decided, right at that moment, that she would have to go see Mxolisi as soon as possible, to sort a few things out.

Mavis tried to keep herself busy for a while, trying to catch up with all the work at Marike's house. As Liziwe was working her way through the backlog of dishes, Mavis was cleaning the rest of the house, and when she was done, she loaded all the house laundry into a washing machine. Liziwe had never seen a machine that washes clothes in her life! In fact just about everything in this house was very different to what she was used to.

After about three to four hours of doing this and that in the house, Mavis walked into the kitchen to check on Liziwe. And she was surprised. Not only did Liziwe properly wash and dry the dishes, she had packed them nicely as she had been told, and had swept and mopped the kitchen floor. The place was spotless.

Mavis smiled. She looked at Liziwe and suddenly thought of her own daughter Lizeka. They were so alike! The only difference was perhaps the fact that Liziwe seemed much keener to learn. Mavis broke the silence after a while, and said, "We're almost done now. I'm just waiting for the washing to come out of the machine. Thereafter I will do the ironing. In the meantime there's somewhere I need to go to. Finish up here and then go and relax." "Oh ok, I'm done too", said Liziwe.

Mavis left Marike's house for a while to see Mxolisi, her boyfriend. Mxolisi worked as a 'garden boy' in the same street, four houses away from where Mavis worked. Theirs was an on and off, sometimes turbulent affair which, against all odds, had lasted over three years now.

As she arrived at the back gate of the house where Mxolisi worked, Mavis became worried about how he would take what she was about to tell him. But it needed to be done. She steeled herself.

After a brief exchange of greetings, characterized by surreptitious looks and understated awareness of the physical connection between them, Mavis said, "Sorry to disturb you at work like this, but I need to talk to you urgently."

Mxolisi replied, sensing the urgency of the matter, "Alright, alright, Mantsundu, what's up?" He listened attentively as Mavis was relating the news of the arrival of Mandla's children. His face was deadpan, betraying no emotion whatsoever.

Only when he spoke did Mavis realize that he was in fact enraged. Looking straight into Mavis's eyes, he said, with a quiet voice, "We have a child, you know", and continued before Mavis could say anything in response, "I will not be a father to Mandla's children, and so I ask you, where does this put me, Nobahle?"

Mxolisi called her by her real name only when he was angry at her. Otherwise he called either 'Hlehle' or by her clan name 'MaNtsundu'. Sometimes, when he was in a mischievous mood he would call her by her employment name of 'Mavis'. His anger right now was caused by the seeming fact that he would still not be rid of Mandla no matter how dead the man was!

"Where does this put us, you ask?" said Mavis taking a deep sigh. Looking at Mxolisi directly, she said,

"I came here to tell you that, under the circumstances, you and me, cannot be. I cannot, in good conscience, ask you to be a part of this. This is an issue whose

> *impact is likely to last a lifetime. I cannot therefore*
> *ask you to wait for me. You have your own life to*
> *lead, and it's only fair that we end things at this*
> *point. I hope, for the sake of Phikolomzi, we shall*
> *remain friends."*

Mavis stopped talking, and seemed to be waiting for a response from Mxolisi. But Mxolisi too remained quiet for some time, just looking at Mavis without blinking an eye, and then at last he said, "I agree my sister."

Again, 'my sister' was a form of sarcasm which Mxolisi sometimes used when upset. He continued,

> *"I cannot be part of this. As you say, you and me,*
> *cannot be. Of course this does not make you my*
> *enemy, although I would prefer it if we didn't see*
> *each other from now on. I shall find a way in which*
> *I can continue to support Phikolomzi without*
> *having to fraternize with you. Now if you are done,*
> *I would like to return to my work."*

Mavis replied as she at the same was turning around to leave, "Yes, as a matter of fact I am done. Good bye." She then left through the same back gate she had come in through earlier, leaving Mxolisi behind seething with anger.

In fact, as it was, Mxolisi had been preparing to take his relationship with Mavis to the next level. He had already sent word out to his relatives that he had seen a woman; that it was serious; and they should be ready for the talks with her relatives.

Now this! 'The first thing *nje* that happens on a Monday is that I get dumped! Bloody hell!' He muttered, as he increasingly became animated. He restarted the petrol lawnmower which he had been using before being interrupted by Mavis. With the motor running, he started pacing up and down, pushing the lawnmower on the grass – without really looking at whether or not any grass was being cut, all the while still talking to himself, "You think you know somebody! And then they turn around and betray you like this. *Tyhini madoda! Ngoku ndiyahamba kwalapha!* She will never ever see me again!'

But as far as Mavis was concerned, this was all for the best. As she left Mxolisi behind in a livid state, she was thinking, that perhaps certain things are best left unsaid. It was enough that she had ended the affair with Mxolisi, over her unofficial adoption of Mandla's children. But what Mxolisi didn't know, a fact that would otherwise drive him over the dark edge, was that even Phikolomzi, the three year old child he was claiming as his, was in fact Mandla's.

SECTION FIVE

SECTION FIVE

THE KINDNESS OF STRANGERS

"What's wrong Mari?" Fred asked, looking at his wife, with concern in his voice, as he observed a seemingly absently minded Marike. She was just sitting on the couch and staring into the distance, and she did not immediately respond to Fred's question. Instead, she turned around and looked at her husband for a few seconds, and then said, "Well, I'm fine actually. I'm just having a lot on my mind." Fred did not probe further, limiting his response merely to saying, "In that case, I'll be outside. Got a lot of stuff to do too."

It had now been two days since the Ncadana children arrived. Although she would hate to admit it, but Marike Le Roux was clearly fascinated by Liziwe. Having listened to the story of why and how she left home, and how she got to choose to travel, with her young siblings from the Transkei to Roodepoort, made her wonder about what kind of creatures children really are. It was something that also made her to think about how her own children would have been, had she been blessed with them.

She and Fred did not have children. After years of trying, doctors finally confirmed that she was infertile. They had thought of adopting but they never could fully commit to the idea. Now both of them at seventy five years old, they had become comfortable in their own company as spinsters.

But the sudden arrival of Liziwe and her siblings at her house, had the effect of reviving Marike's unfulfilled wish of having children. Remembering what Mavis had earlier said, that she would take the children with to Dobsonville the next time she gets her off day, she was struck by an idea. Sitting on one of the settees in her lounge, she felt a well of excitement growing inside as the idea took hold. She stood up, with a painful grunt, and limped over to the Kitchen where Mavis was washing dishes, and she said, "Mavis will you please make me Fred a cup of tea, please."

This was strange, Mavis thought. Normally whenever Marike wanted coffee or tea, she would just want it for herself only, and Fred would also do the same thing. But they seldom sat down, the two of them for tea.

As soon as Mavis put a tray containing tea cups, a kettle and a sugar basin on the lounge coffee table, Marike called Fred over. "Fred honey, come here. We need to talk", she said.

Fred, who was busy cleaning his shotgun outside under a tree, was mildly puzzled and slightly irritated by this disturbance. 'What on earth could she be wanting to talk to me about now? Can't she see I'm busy here?!' He grumbled to himself. But in spite of himself, he slowly walked over to the living room where Marike was. "What's so important that it can't wait?" He asked casually.

"Well", said Marike, "I'll just come out and say it."

"I wouldn't prefer it any other way", said Fred, interrupting her.

She just waved her hand, as if appealing for him not to interrupt, and continued, "About what we were talking about earlier, you know, that we must choose a charity on which we must bestow some of our money and possessions …"

Again Fred interjected, "You do know that this 'earlier' you're talking about is in fact three years ago, right?!"

Marike did not respond to this, except by just giving her husband a look, as in 'will you stop already!' She continued, "I've been thinking about that today, and I think we now need to do something for sure, instead of always postponing things."

Fred asked, once more interrupting her, "What do you have in mind dear?"

"It's the children who walked in here two days ago. There's something I find particularly touching about them. For one thing, they took a big risk coming here."

"Yeah, that they did", said Fred, "But I still don't get why you want us to talk about them now."

"My point is", Marike continued, "we have to recognize the hand of God in this."

"But darling", said Fred, raising his hand in demurred protest, "I don't know where you're headed with this, but just in case you didn't notice, they're black! By law we can't keep them. Do you know how much trouble we would be in? The Group Areas inspectors can show up here at any time and demand to see who works here. How do you propose we explain having three black children in the house?!"

"I know", Marike said, "there's probably a myriad of laws prohibiting the provision of support to black people. But hear me out. I didn't say we would keep them. But let us encourage Mavis to. We can buy a house for Mavis in Dobsonville where she would stay with the children, and we could establish an education trust for all the children in her care. They can go to schools in the township or in the rural areas where it's more peaceful. Effectively what I'm saying is, let us help them."

Fred took a few seconds before saying anything, and then slowly he said, "I get that you want to help, and indeed we are in a position to offer that help. What I don't get is why these kids. It's not as if you've not seen children before, and there are millions of destitute black kids all over town."

"You haven't noticed, have you?" Marike asked, "The children, especially the older one, bears a striking resemblance to Mavis's daughter. Call it telepathy, but I call it fate. Fate is bringing the children together, and I think we must support that. I can't begin to imagine the crisis of conscious that Mavis is going through right now, and we've been talking about rewarding her for being loyal to us all these years. No man Fred, let's do this!"

For a while, Fred remained silent, just looking into the distance. He and Marike, rich as they were, lived very simple lives. She had her own interests and things that kept her busy, which included knitting and crocheting, pruning flowers in the garden, playing word puzzles and reading magazines. For his part, Fred mostly occupied his time with fixing stuff around the house. It's only on Sundays that they would both go to church.

As far as Fred was concerned, up to this point the arrival of the Ncadana children was none of his business. He had not paid any particular attention to what had happened to them since he was briefly introduced to them. But listening to his wife, and seeing how taken up she was by the whole thing, Fred was suddenly attentive, as he said, "Remember how we said we would end things here? And now this thing with Dr Maree, and your diabetes ..." He didn't finish the sentence, and instead he became pensive, as if feeling the weight of what he was saying.

It was now Marike's turn to be suddenly silent. She knew what her husband meant by 'here'. She remembered the covenant they made when they both retired, that as they reach old age, before they become senile and helpless, they would not burden anyone with having to look after them – that they will, both of them, commit suicide by drinking poison.

Marike looked at her husband, with steady eyes and a bland face, wondering how long he'd been thinking about this. She looked again at Fred, as if in concurrence, and then she slowly nodded her head and said, "You're reading my mind dear. I agree, it's time."

"In that case", said Fred, "Let us begin to wind things down. All that you've said now, let's say it in writing – as our last will and testament."

Marike again nodded her head in agreement, and then said, "I'll draw up a draft, which you must check and agree with, and then we'll call Brian to arrange signing."

"Alright baby girl", said Fred with a teasing tone, "Let's drink tea when Mavis is off." He didn't normally use terms of endearment with his wife - only when being sarcastic or deadly serious about something. Marike smiled knowingly, and said, "It's a date darling."

BEGINNING OF
A NEW BEGINNING

It was late in the afternoon of Saturday the 22nd of December 1979, when Mavis arrived back at her house in Dobsonville. Usually she would be exhausted at this time, especially when she arrives at home. But she wasn't, and she credited the support given by Liziwe in doing some of the work at Marike's house.

'Liziwe! My God!' Her mind still boggled each time she thought about the week's events. It was a week which she could only describe as perhaps the most interesting, if not downright tumultuous, she had ever had. It had been a week in which she changed her life dramatically, without any guarantee that it was for the better. In fact every time she looked at Liziwe and her siblings, she wondered what was going to happen from hereon, and whether she had made the right decision in allowing them to stay with her.

Although by township standards, her house was actually not a 'big house' - a phrase often used to describe township matchbox houses which had been extended, it was nonetheless a big four roomed house, with an unused shack at the back. Mavis often rented out the shack to make additional income for herself. But for now it stood empty, mainly because she did not want strangers around her three year old baby son, Phikolomzi.

Today Mavis was coming home because the following day, which was a Sunday, was her off day. She was expected back at Marike's house first thing on Monday, the Christmas Eve of 1979. How she wished she could have more time to spend at home with her children! In fact she always resented having to go on a break for only one day in a week. But alas, as she herself would put it, '*ijob'ijob*!'

At just after six in the afternoon, it was already dark, a fact made more so by the smog engulfing the township, which was coming from a million Dova coal stoves all throughout Soweto. Unlike previous times, today Mavis arrived at her house not only with a bag of goodies from the madam's house. She had three children with her.

Lizeka, Mavis's nine year old daughter, who had been impatiently waiting for her mother's return for quite a while already, saw them coming a distance away. The three children with her mother threw her off at first. But she could see that these were not the usual children from the neighbourhood, who would also mob her mother, begging her for sweets – these were actually with her mother.

When Mavis saw Lizeka standing near the fence, she called her over, "Hey Lizeka, what's wrong with you? Don't just stand there. Come and help me with this stuff." Lizeka opened the gate and walked over to her mother, and took two grocery filled plastic bags from her. All the while she was looking at Liziwe with undisguised puzzlement, and all the way to the house, Lizeka never took her eyes off Liziwe.

As they got inside the house, Mavis put everything down on the floor and directed the three children to sit down on the sofas in the sparsely furnished lounge, which also doubled as a dining room. She then turned to Lizeka and said, "Hey LK, as you can see, we have visitors."

Lizeka interjected by asking, smiling, and her eyes darting about, "Who are they mama?"

"Well", said Mavis with a sigh, "to cut a long story short, this is Liziwe, your sister. This here is Tembisa, your other sister, and this is Ntando, your second brother." Mavis paused, deliberately. She wanted Lizeka to get that she was not speaking church language when she said these were her sisters and brother.

To say Lizeka was confused would be an understatement. She just looked at Mavis, searching for meaning. Mavis could hear her little mind working, trying to make sense of it all, and then, as if somehow she's convinced herself that she understood, she broke into a broad smile. For Mavis, it was all she needed. She had dreaded Lizeka's reaction when told that she had siblings she had had no prior knowledge of. Of course Mavis knew that Lizeka could still react negatively to this later on.

But for now, Mavis was relieved, and she said, "OK LK, I know you have questions. I'll tell you all you need to know some other time. For now let's make everybody comfortable. I see Phiko is asleep. Don't disturb him."

Liziwe too was relieved, not just by Lizeka's friendly disposition, but at the fact that they had now come to a place where there was more freedom and space to move about, which was just not there at Marike's house. The irony of appreciating freedom in a township was of course totally lost on Liziwe. She'd never been in a township before, and she was curious about everything, and Mavis and Lizeka were there, ready to show her around.

In fact Mavis spent the entire Sunday talking to the children, about how Liziwe, Tembisa and Ntando took a trip to Roodepoort; how she knew their father Mandla; and how they must always be together because they are related.

As part of her Christmas shopping, she showed them around Soweto. Their trip included a train ride from the nearby Ikwezi Station to New Canada, and then a taxi to the Black Chain mall in Diepkloof. After briefly shopping for cheap clothes at the stands outside the mall, they took a taxi to 'town' –to the Carlton Centre in Johannesburg. Liziwe was of course to learn that even though all the places she had seen looked like a town, the term 'town' actually was reserved for the Johannesburg CBD. By the end of the day, they were all dog tired, but with plenty of stories to tell.

SILENCE AT THE HOUSE
OF THE LE ROUXS

On Monday the 24th of December 1979, Mavis woke up very early in the morning and prepared to report for duty at the Le Roux's house. She could feel it in her body. The Christmas bug had well and truly struck. Even this early, people were up and rushing to town for last minute shopping. That it was actually raining cats and dogs was totally of no consequence.

But alas. For Mavis it would not be such a festive season. She would spend her Christmas not with her family, but working at the Le Roux's. Today however, she drew solace from the fact that for the first time she was less anxious about leaving Lizeka and Phikolomzi alone. She had a good sense, that with Liziwe as the grown up, the children and the house were in very good hands indeed. In fact she thought it was remarkable that both Liziwe and Lizeka shared similar life experiences, because just as Liziwe had had the responsibility of looking after Tembisa and Ntando for as long as she could remember, Lizeka too had to look after the three year old Phikolomzi and their house for most of the week while Mavis was away at work.

Mavis left for work dejected at the fact that she was leaving her family behind on Christmas Eve, but with her spirits up all the same. She felt a sense of accomplishment she had never known before. She stood in the rain for a while, waiting for a taxi alongside the street just in front of her house. But she did not have to wait for long as many Dobsonville taxis were up and already making a brisk trade – rushing last minute Christmas shoppers to Johannesburg and to Roodepoort. In no time, and without even paying attention to the road, the taxi arrived at the gate of the Le Roux's house.

But as soon as she alighted from the taxi in front of Marike's house, Mavis could sense that something was amiss. The house was in total darkness. Mavis thought this was strange. Fred always insisted on keeping every outside light on during the night, and they would remain on until he wakes up and switches them off. Mavis approached the kitchen entrance she always used with some trepidation, not sure what to expect.

And sure enough, as soon as she opened the kitchen door, she was met by a wafting smell of what she only knew too well - death. Instinctively, experience told her what this meant. But she denied it, refusing to believe that her mind could think of something so ghastly. But then, what could it be? She asked herself. The Le Roux's did not have any pets, so it was unlikely that a dog or a cat had died.

She looked around the kitchen with a growing sense of unease. The kitchen was clean, pretty much the same way she left it when she went off duty on Saturday afternoon. This was unusual. She called out for Marike, "Madam! Madam! Madam!" But there was no reply. Slowly, carefully she walked over to the lounge area. This seemed to be where the smell was coming from. And then her eyes popped out of their sockets when she saw the scene in the lounge. There they were, both Marike and Fred were slumped on the settees - dead.

She screamed. It was an involuntary reaction, and she put her hand on her mouth. Careful not to touch anything, Mavis rushed back to the kitchen. She knew that Marike kept a list of emergency numbers pinned on the fridge door. But before should could look at the list, she was distracted. There was a note pinned on the door next to the numbers list. She looked at it, and it read: *"Dear Mavis, call Captain Van Huyssteen of the Roodepoort Police. He'll know what to do. His number is on the list. Marike and Fred."*

After placing the call to Captain Van Huyssteen, who promised to arrive at the house as soon as possible, Mavis went outside and to her room at the back. At the back of her mind she was hoping to see Albert, Marike's gardener, who had only been a month with the Le Roux's. But as it was, Albert had also gone off duty at the same time with Mavis, and was also expected to be back today. So he was not yet in. Mavis thought about telling the neighbours about what had happened, but decided against it. Marike and Fred had kept to themselves for most of their lives, and they had no relatives.

About twenty minutes later, a police vehicle pulled up in front of the Le Roux house, and Captain Van Huyssteen got out. He was a tall bulky fellow with biceps and a big moustache, Mavis noticed. He was accompanied by three young white police officers, all looking like fresh recruits, with their uniforms looking new and their hair crew cut. As they alighted out of the van, Mavis noticed that they were carrying two stretchers.

As soon as he saw Mavis, Van Huyssteen approached her and growled, with a thick Afrikaans accent, "*Is jou naam Mavis?*" Mavis replied, in broken Afrikaans, "*Ja Baas, kom hierdie kant asseblief.*" She showed him where the lounge was. "*Baie dankie,* I'll take it from here." He said, waving her away.

A while later, Van Huyssteen emerged from the lounge, and found Mavis still standing outside in the front yard of the house, looking dazed and confused. He said,

> *"Well I'm done. My guys are now taking them to morgue. At this stage we don't suspect any foul play. It looks like they drank tea laced with poison. Of course the lab will have to confirm that for sure. I'll inform their family attorney, Mr Brian Cooling, and he'll lead things from there on. I suggest you stick around for a while until you hear from him, ok?"*

Mavis nodded her head, and watched as the young police officers were loading the bodies of her employers to the back of their van, covered in black plastic bags. The scene was surreal, and it got Mavis to think about how strange this whole drama was — that it had no anti-climax! Instead of cooking a storm in Marike's kitchen, preparing for Christmas Day, she was now stuck between doing nothing and going home! She just sat on one of the kitchen stools, resting her face on her hands, and pondering her future. 'But God, will you make me understand exactly what it is you want?! First, you just drop children on my lap, and then take away my employers! What do you want me to do?!' Mavis exclaimed with exasperation.

She sat in the kitchen, wallowing in her thoughts, for about two hours, and then the phone rang. It startled her, and she nearly fell off the chair. But she soon composed herself, and answered it.

On the line it was the voice of a stranger, a man, and as soon as she picked up, the man said, "Are you Mavis?"

"Yes", replied Mavis, noting the man's English accent.

"My name is Brian Cooling. We need to talk. Can I send somebody to come get you?"

"What is this about?" Mavis asked, her mind racing, wondering what was going on.

"It concerns your employers. I'll tell you all about it when you get here. Within the next thirty minutes someone will come pick you up, OK?" Brian did not wait for Mavis to agree. He just dropped the line, and Mavis was left exclaiming, "Amen!"

Indeed, about thirty minutes later, a white Toyota Cressida pulled up at the front gate, and the driver got out. It was a black middle aged, neat and cleanly shaven man. As soon as he saw Mavis standing in the doorway looking at him, he approached and said, "My name is Bongani. I've been sent here by Mr Cooling to take you to his office. Please come with me ma'am."

"OK, but just wait a minute", Mavis said, and she mumbled to herself, 'Strange day this!' She then locked the house and got into Bongani's car, and they drove off to Johannesburg. About thirty minutes later, Mavis arrived at the sixteenth floor offices of Brian Cooling Attorneys in Prichard Street in the centre of Johannesburg. Bongani led her into a big boardroom, with a large oblong shaped table which had about eighteen black rocking leather chairs. Bongani asked her to wait there.

Mavis waited in this room for about five minutes, looking at a string of portraits of white elderly men adorning the wall. And then a short and bald man, wearing black pants, a white shirt with rolled up sleeves and a black tie, walked in, and quickly introduced himself, self-assuredly. "Hi, my name is Brian Cooling. Thank you for coming. I'll make this short."

Mavis could see that this was not going to be a conversation. She had questions, chief among which was why she had been brought here in the first place. But she resisted the temptation to ask, seeing that Brian would likely not allow her anyway. Indeed Brian did not waste any time, and started by saying,

> *"Marike and Fred will be buried at the Roodepoort Cemetery this afternoon. There will be no big service or anything, just a quiet little affair. You're welcome to be part of it. It will just be me and the municipal cemetery staff. As you know, they did not have any relatives. But the reason I called you here is to read to you their will. It was their wish that it be read to you. I know this probably should wait until after the funeral. But I'm flying to New York tomorrow evening and I will not be back till the end of March next year. So if you'll allow me, here's Fred and Marike Le Roux's last will and testament."*

Mavis was confused. But she bit her lip. She listened attentively as Brian read out Fred and Marike's will:

> *We, the undersigned, Fred and Marike Le Roux, spouses married in community of property and*

presently residing at no 114 Ontdekkers Road, Florida, do hereby revoke all previous will, codicils and any other testamentary dispositions previously made by us, and declare the following to be our last Will and Testament:

We bequeath the sum of our estate made up as follows: the house and all its contents, which is at no 114 Ontdekkers Road, Florida; two farms in the Orange Free State province, one in Bethlehem, and the other in Senekal; monies in bank accounts at Allied Bank and Trust Bank to the tune R1.7 million; shares in companies reflected in the attachment hereof, amounting to R7 million; insurance policies with Adsure Assurers, amounting to R40 million, and our pension monies held by Sansure totalling R2.5 million.

Accordingly, we hereby direct Brian Coolings Attorneys to establish a trust where all the aforementioned assets will be held, and we nominate Ms Mavis Nobahle Nxego (hereafter Mavis) as the sole beneficiary.

Brian Coolings Attorneys is further directed to ensure that Mavis uses the money and all the assets to support the educational and welfare needs of all the children in her care. This provision is limited exclusively to the following children, namely Lizeka Nxego, Phikolomzi Nxego, Liziwe Ncadana, Tembisa Ncadana, and Ntando Ncadana. It is further directed that Mavis may, on her discretion, add further beneficiaries in this regard but not exceeding three.

We are mindful of the fact that the laws of our country currently prohibit the settlement of

black people in areas demarcated for whites only.
It is not our purpose here to argue the correctness
or otherwise of these laws. Suffice it to say that,
should this situation change, as we think it will,
Brian Coolings Attorneys is directed to cede the
ownership of the property at no 114 Ontdekkers
Road, to Mavis. Should Mavis be deceased by this
time, the oldest of the children currently under her
care should be given the ownership of the property,
under the proviso that she/he shares it with all
surviving children previously cared for by Mavis. In
the meantime, Brian Coolings Attorneys is directed
to immediately effect improvements as may be
necessary to Mavis's house in Dobsonville.

Lastly, Brian Coolings is directed to make
gratuity payment of twenty thousand rand to our
gardener, Albert Morosi.

Signed in the presence of the undersigned
witnesses, all being present at the same time, at
Johannesburg on 24 December day of 1979

When Brian was done, he took off his reading glasses and looked up, at Mavis, and said, "Well, here we are Ms Nxego! If you are agree with this, I'm required to ask you to sign here, and then everything will become effective immediately."

Mavis, quite easily the most talkative person in the world, was at a loss for words. She was not even aware that she was crying until Brian offered her a box Kleenex tissues. She kept mumbling to herself, totally oblivious to the presence of Brian in the room, "What has God done now?! What has He done now?!" At last she finally managed to gather her senses, and slowly picked up the ballpoint pen offered by Brian, and signed.

Brian, with characteristic understatement, then said, "That's that then. Let's go to the funeral service, shall we?"

AFFAIRS SET IN ORDER

It was in the middle of January 1980, and schools all over Soweto were opening. Fresh faced children – girls in shiny Jim dresses and boys in grey pants and white shirts, were lining the streets, going to their various schools. It was a picture of systemic chaos, with the air of gay abundance and hope reflected in the faces of some of the children balanced in equal measure by the highly charged political atmosphere in Soweto and elsewhere in the country, with some of the children seemingly loitering instead of purposefully going to school.

Normally Mavis would be frustrated at having to stand in long queues at school trying to register Lizeka, to get books and to shop around for school uniforms. But this time she was actually relieved. Even though the death of her employers had gifted her the Christmas she did not think she would have, it was not exactly a holiday. She was still having sleepless nights, still unable to accept the fact that overnight her life had changed as a result of the generous inheritance she received from her employers.

Today, with the main street in Dobsonville clogged with traffic, and the sidewalks filled with children of all ages, Mavis was looking forward to the opening of schools, not only to escape from her own thoughts and the excitement of suddenly being rich, but because with the exception of the three year old Phikolomzi, all the children would be going to school.

With Liziwe, Lizeka, Tembisa and Ntando in tow, Mavis excitedly joined hundreds of other parents hoping to register their children at the J Simelane Primary School. She was unperturbed by the fact that all the parents waiting in front of the school's administration block were nervous and concerned about the future of their children - not so much about what they ultimately would become, but about whether they would get education at all. The politics of the country were completely unpredictable, with riots taking place in all the black townships of the Transvaal. As it was, some of the parents were already ditching township schools and were prepared to pay extra money for transport and tuition at private schools in the Johannesburg city centre. But as far as Mavis was concerned, all she wanted was to take the children to school, and if it didn't work at this particular school, she would take them to another one.

Having completed the process of filling forms and all the children having been assigned to classes, Mavis pulled Liziwe aside, and said, "Well, here we are kid. You said you wanted this. Make it count."

The look of sheer determination in Liziwe's eyes was all the convincing Mavis needed. In fact Liziwe's class teacher, Mrs Doreen Mokoena remarked on Liziwe's first quarter report at the end of March that year, that *'Liziwe is one of the most keen pupils I've ever had the pleasure of teaching. With support and encouragement, she will go far.'*

For Liziwe, her siblings and her newfound sister and friend Lizeka, this was the start of a new life. From now on they would spend their lives totally immersed into their school work, and with funding from the inheritance received from Fred and Marike Le Roux, Mavis had no worries – not on this score.

But, all the same Mavis did have other worries. A year after the arrival of Liziwe and her siblings, she started to feel her own health faltering. She was very happy at the way things have turned out, especially at the promising progress the children were making with their school work, and at the special bond that had developed between Liziwe and Lizeka.

All of them in their own ways were enriching her life beyond measure. The inheritance from the Le Roux's had made all the difference and given her a peace of mind. She had told the children everything they needed to know, about herself - where she grew up, where she went to school, when she came to Johannesburg, how she met with Mandla and Mxolisi, how she acquired the house at Dobsonville, when she started working for the Le Roux's, and everything else they wanted to know.

She had never thought it possible, but her house in Dobsonville had truly become a happy place, made more so by the extensions funded by her late employers, Fred and Marike Le Roux. Whichever way she looked at it, God had answered every one of her prayers.

But lately, as she started to feel her energy wasting away, she also began to feel bothered by her breakup with Mandla. His subsequent illness and death had affected her immensely, a fact compounded by the arrival of his orphaned children. She had blamed herself for being selfish in kicking Mandla out of their house as soon as he lost his job due to illness. Perhaps, she thought, Mandla would have regained his health if she had not picked fights with him for not leaving his wife, and for not properly supporting Lizeka. He would have had a stronger motivation to live if he knew that young Phikolomzi was his son, instead of thinking this was the outcome of her other affair with Mxolisi. Quite why she never told either of the men the truth – to Mandla, that this was his son, and to Mxolisi that this was in fact not his son, she could never say, other than simply that 'it is complicated.'

What Mavis also did not tell the children, figuring that they would not know how to handle the information anyway, was that she was sick, and had been at more or less the same that Mandla also got sick. She did not tell them that, just as she knew what had killed Mandla, she too was afflicted by 'the big disease'. She did not tell them that she knew, and was fully expecting that she too was going to die sooner rather than later. Part of her own reticence in this regard was occasioned by the fact that it was an inevitability which she gradually was coming to terms with. She was immensely concerned, and did not know how to tell the children this, that they would soon be alone - with Liziwe, Tembisa and Ntando experiencing this for the second time in their lives.

Thinking about this made Mavis to appreciate for the first time, Liziwe's strong character, for that would soon be called upon to save the situation should the inevitable occur. Suddenly Mavis became uncomfortable. As much as she was gradually beginning to accept the inevitability of her own death, she had not given much thought to its impact to those who would remain behind.

Suddenly gripped by panic, she stood up, with the support of a walking stick. Her whole body was sore, and she had very little energy left in her. But the sense of fear energised her. The last time she went to a doctor in Roodepoort, she was told that her CD4 count was dangerously low, at 210. The doctor had said should it reach below 200, she would have to be admitted to hospital.

But today she was determined to stand up and to catch a taxi to Ikwezi. She wanted to speak to her friend Nomaza Makhuzeni. Although people were not talking, beyond the whispers, about this dreaded "big disease", she and Nomaza had confided to each other. Sometimes they would laugh about it, and reminisce about their 'conquests'. But sometimes they would cry on one another's shoulders.

Mavis of course could still not get over the fact that even though she and Nomaza had moved in the same circles, and had as a matter of fact shared men in the past, Nomaza remained unaffected by the disease. They had talked several times about this, with Mavis cursing her fate, and Nomaza appreciating her 'luck', which she always qualified by 'for now'.

When she arrived at Nomaza's backyard shack, Mavis found Nomaza washing her clothes just in front of the shack. Seeing Nomaza working through a pile of laundry made Mavis to realize that it was in fact a Saturday, and that she could have made the trip for nothing, because she did not even check if Nomaza would be in.

After a brief exchange of pleasantries, Mavis then said,

"Hey Zaza my friend, you may be wondering why I'm here, especially in my current state. So I'll just come out and say it. As you can see, and as you know, I'm dying. Please let's not cry about it now … I need your help. You and I arrived at this Egoli at almost the same time, and we have been friends since.

131

My request is simple. If you agree, I would like you and your sons, Zolani and Shepard to move out of this shack and come and live with us. I have a big house now, and I would like nothing more than to know that my dear friend is looking after it when I'm gone. More importantly I want you to be a figurehead for my children. I don't want my children to do what you and I did, and I can think of no better teacher.

You will not need to do anything about their education and upkeep. All arrangements have been made, and if you agree, these arrangements will be amended to accommodate your sons as well. I just need you to be there with the with the children, guide them to do good, to society and to God."

After a long silence, Nomaza said, with tears in her eyes flowing freely, "Oh Mantsundu! This is so unexpected! You are too kind. Indeed I accept."

"In that case", said Mavis, "you must come to the house tomorrow, I shall introduce you to the children. I'm seeing my doctor two days from now, and chances are I shall be admitted. After that, who knows..."

Nomaza did not say anything else. She was still crying, and shaking her head in amazement. Mavis again continued, trying to break the uneasy silence that had somehow descended, and said, "Tshomi, I see you need a moment to compose yourself. Let me leave you now. I look forward to seeing you at the house tomorrow."

Nomaza nodded her head as she proceeded to help Mavis to stand up, and she then accompanied her to the gate and bid her good bye.

Indeed as Mavis had predicted, when she saw Dr Van Heerden the following day in Roodepoort, he instructed that she be admitted at the Leratong Hospital, which was just outside the township of Kagiso in Krugersdorp. A day after being admitted, the children accompanied by Nomaza paid her a visit. She was awake when they arrived. Nomaza noticed that she was alert though clearly still very weak. They had put her in the TB section of the hospital, Nomaza noticed, in a ward with about twelve other patients.

When she saw them coming into the ward, Mavis could afford a weak by broad smile, and she beckoned for them to come over and sit on the bed next to her, and she said, giving Nomaza and the children a panning look,

"Thank you Zaza! You guys, you all look beautiful. It's good that you've come at this time, otherwise a few minutes later you'd have found me sleeping. The doctors have given me sedative tablets which will shortly be taking effect. I'm so pleased you are all here, because I've been meaning to talk to all of you, but with everything that has been happening in my life I've not had the time to.

I know you are learning all sorts of things at school. I've seen your school reports. I am immensely proud of all you. Of course I cannot teach you the stuff they teach at your school. But because I love you so dearly, and because I want you to make your own mistakes and not to repeat mine, I'll tell you this: I have AIDS. That is what is killing me – the Acquired Immune Deficiency Syndrome. Learn about it, and take all the necessary steps to avoid contracting it. My own situation is now in God's hands. I may come out of this hospital, but then again I may not. Whatever happens I want you to know that you now have each other. God, in his infinite wisdom, has brought you together.

All I want to say, before I fall asleep, is that you must support one another. You must work together as a family. You must love one another as blood relatives. My friend Nomaza here will guide you. But in the end, you yourselves must live your own lives in the best manner possible."

Indeed Mavis could barely finish the last sentence before she closed her eyes and dozed off. The nurse urged them out of the hospital ward, imploring them to come back on the next visiting hours.

As they left the hospital, they were all quiet. Nomaza could sense that even though the children didn't know what this AIDS was, they had received the message to learn about it, and avoid its ravaging impact. Nomaza could still not believe her friend's courage in talking to children about a matter every other adult would rather die keeping it a secret rather than risk being shamed by family and friends.

Two days later, Nomaza broke the news to Liziwe, Lizeka and Tembisa, that Mavis had passed on. Needless to say, the death of Mavis hit the children very hard. Everyone of them had seen Mavis being sick and struggling to even walk. But none of them even thought of the possibility that she would be gone from their lives so soon. Lizeka was particularly struck by this loss. She cried for most the day when the news first broke out. Nomaza had of course been more aware than the children of this impending disaster and tried her level best to calm Lizeka down and to console the rest of the children. And she looked to Liziwe for support.

A few days later, after informing Brian Coolings about the news of the death of Mavis, which Mavis in her last days had instructed her to do, Nomaza set about arranging the funeral. In fact, after discussions with both Lizeka and Liziwe, they decided that Mavis would be buried at Dobsonville Cemetery.

SECTION SIX

A PASSAGE OF TIME

In the days and months following the death of Mavis, Liziwe, working with Nomaza Makhuzeni worked tirelessly to ensure that the house and the children were properly cared for. The death of Mavis affected Liziwe in much the same way that it affected Lizeka, Mavis's daughter. She had not known Mavis for long, but in the short period she had been with her at her house in Dobsonville, a bond had begun to develop between the two of them.

Subsequently, and all throughout her life, Liziwe would always have fond memories of the times when she and Mavis talked for long hours about her father, mainly about how they met. She was fascinated by how frank Mavis was about everything, especially matters concerning romantic relationships involving grown-ups. She recalled moments when she was spellbound by listening to Mavis narrating the story of how she, her mother Nonzame and her father Mandla were in a love triangle – with Mavis being the Joburg 'fling' as she put it, and her mother being Mandla's rural country sweetheart.

She remembered listening with feeling as Mavis narrated the pain, shock and anger when Mandla made his choice to marry Nonzame instead of her. And she listened with amazement as Mavis told her that, even though the relationship continued long after the marriage, it was never the same. The spark had gone, but they kept at it for the sake of her daughter, Lizeka, until she eventually decided to terminate it when it became clear that Mandla would never leave his wife.

Liziwe remembered being told by Mavis, that they must take time and find out more about their father Mandla. It was therefore part of following up on what Mavis had said that Liziwe also decided, six months after Mavis's death, to visit her father's backyard shack, which was within an easy walking distance from Mavis's house.

Accompanied by Lizeka and Tembisa, Liziwe arrived at the house where her father had lived before falling sick and deciding to go home. As she approached the house, which was a typical match box township house, with a small but immaculate front yard lawn, she saw an elder sixty something lady. This was Mrs Khumulo, the owner of the house, and she was busy polishing the front stoep of the house with red Cobra polish. On seeing Liziwe standing at the gate, Mrs Khumalo stood up and said, "Come in my children. *Ngenani,* the gate is not locked. Who are you?"

But before Liziwe could respond, Mrs Khumalo started to clap her hands as if suddenly seeing something amazing. She was looking at both Liziwe and Lizeka, her eyes panning from the one to the other of the two siblings, all the while exclaiming, "Amen! I'll be damned! Don't tell me, you kids are Mandla's children!!"

"Yes mama, we are! How did you guess?!" Liziwe asked, looking at her sister Lizeka, amazed.

"Guess?" Mrs Khumalo asked, "No, you kids, both of you look exactly like Mandla! Come in, come in! Can

I offer you anything to drink, or eat? How is Mandla? I know he was unwell the last time I saw him. And then he just disappeared!"

At the same as Mrs Khumalo was talking, she dropped everything else she was doing, and also ushered Liziwe and Lizeka to the lounge area of her four roomed house. As they sat down, it was Liziwe again who spoke, and said, "No mama, thank you for the offer, but we're fine really. About my father, Mandla, well that is why we are here mama. My name is Liziwe, and this here is my sister, Lizeka. My father died in December last year. We wanted to see if there some of his stuff here."

Mrs Khumalo replied, "Oh I'm sorry to hear that! He was such a gentleman, your father." Liziwe interjected, excitedly, "How well did you know him?"

"Well", replied Mrs Khumalo,

"As much as anyone can know one's tenant really. He kept to himself. Even though he drank, I never had any trouble with him. Of course it may not be your business. After all you're just kids. But you know, he was also quite a ladies man! Every weekend, he would either not sleep at his shack, or he would bring with him a strange woman. I scolded him at some point about this. But he would just laugh at me! He spoke about you all the time, you know – 'Liziwe this, Lizeka that, and 'Ntando that'. He had big dreams, especially about your education. In fact as I recall, he even took a comprehensive education policy for all his children. He used to complain about how he would cope with monthly payments. But he was so dedicated

*to this all the same. Oh and I also remember being
irritated at him for bringing all sorts of building
stuff into my yard, and whenever I asked him why
he was collecting these things, he would say he's
preparing to build his house in the Transkei! Indeed
there are some of his things in storage at the garage.
I took them out of the shack when saw that he was
not coming back. I needed the shack, but I would
appreciate it if you could take all of them with you.
I do need that space too now."*

When Mrs Khumalo was done talking, she asked Liziwe
and Lizeka to follow her to the garage where Mandla's stuff
was kept. As they moved towards the garage, Liziwe was
looking around the house, and she saw that there were three
shacks at the back, and at the doorway of each there were
women, probably tenants or wives and girlfriends of the
tenants. They were just standing there, curiously looking at
her and Lizeka, whispering among themselves and making
gestures towards the main house.

As they were busy going through her father's stuff in
the garage, they could hear these ladies gossiping amongst
themselves. Liziwe couldn't make out what their names were
as they kept referring to one another by what she assumed
were nicknames. First she heard 'Ncebsy' saying, "*Wena!
Noba kuth'wa izint' azifani!* These are Mandla's kids, Both
of them are!"

'Dolly', the woman standing in the doorway of the
middle shack, retorted, "Only two my friend?! Can't be!
That man did really sow his wild oats!"

And then Liziwe heard the shocking interjection of
third woman from the shack furthest to the left, whose

name was 'Sistas', saying, "Yho! *Oko ndibajongile tshomi! Ndi'ske ndamangala!* Can you see how both of them look exactly like my Nosipho! *Heee! Ngumhlola*!

"Yho my friend! I didn't want to say anything. But there's a definite resemblance there for sure!" said Ncebsy animatedly.

Sistas replied, looking concerned "Esheee! Maybe I should confirm this for sure. I've my doubts I must say – but, I mean, it was such a brief encounter!"

"Oh yeah?" said Dolly interjecting, "And just how long do you think these 'encounters' should be?!"

Sistas replied, sheepishly, "Ag you know what I mean!"

To Liziwe, and indeed to Lizeka, listening to this conversation was even more revealing about who their father was, good and bad. When they heard the name of 'Nosipho' they looked at each other, both wondering who that was! But they both decided to focus on the matter at hand, even though Liziwe quietly resolved to find out more about this Nosipho who could or could not be her sister!

After quickly going through Mandla's personal effects, which mainly consisted of ploughing equipment, garden implements such as spades, wheelbarrows, and boxes filled with an assortment of tools, both Liziwe and Lizeka made the determination that they did not need any of the stuff. All they took with them was a box filled with papers, mainly correspondence from the burial society Mandla belonged to, pay slips from Durban Deep mine, and the insurance policy documents Mrs Khumalo had spoken about, which showed that Liziwe, Lizeka, Tembisa and Ntando were covered for an amount of R500 000, payable on the death of Mandla Ncadana.

Liziwe briefly wondered why her brother Phikolomzi was not covered by this. But she soon figured that whatever the reason was, it did not matter. She would take the papers to Brian and would advise for the inclusion of Phikolomzi.

When they were done, Liziwe informed Mrs Khumalo, saying, *"Mama Enkosi wethu.* Thank you for talking to us about our father, and thank you for looking after his things. We are done here. We will not be needing of this stuff. If you don't want it, I'll ask my brother Ntando and his friends to fetch and dispose them." Mrs Khumalo replied, "Ag, maybe just leave it where it is my child. Perhaps I can still sell of the stuff. Leave it to me. I take it we are done then?"

Liziwe replied, "Indeed we are mama. We don't live far from here. You are welcome to come and visit anytime you want." "You too my child, thank you!" With that, they, Liziwe and her sister Lizeka left Mrs Khumalo's house feeling more enlightened, yet still curious to know more about who their father was.

As the time went by, and in spite of herself, Liziwe began to feel more at ease with her new environment. She felt herself settling in to life in the township, and began to make new friends. All her worries about the strange place she left her village of Mcuncuzo for, and her concerns about meeting people she absolutely knew nothing about, had now become a wonderful memory.

At the J Simelane Primary School, she took to her school work like fish to water, and quickly cultivated a practice of insisting to Tembisa, Ntando, Lizeka, as well as to Nomaza's children, Zolani and Shepard, not to go to bed without either doing their school work or reading a book. She also insisted that each of the children take turns to read to the young Phikolomzi.

To her pleasant surprise, Nomaza found that in Liziwe she had a partner in managing Mavis's house, and she found Liziwe's growing and uncompromising resolve to focus on getting good school results quite endearing. It was an attitude which Nomaza saw rubbing off on all the other children in the house.

In fact Nomaza was to later concede to herself that her own children, whom she moved with to Mavis's house, would not have been as successful as they later turned out, had it not been for Liziwe's tenacity and positive influence on everyone around her.

Of course, focusing on school and on supporting her siblings did not mean that Liziwe had forgotten about her home back in Mcuncuzo. There were times when she would feel depressed and melancholy, with her mind going back to the death of her parents, the night walk away from home, the people she met along the way, including father Dinga, her fortuitous meeting with Marike and Fred Le Roux, and the person who would later loom the largest in her life, Mavis Nxego.

As she progressed from primary school, high school and university, she learnt to refuse to let herself down. On the days when either Tembisa or Ntando would, out of the blue ask something about home, all Liziwe would emphatically say, "There is nothing there guys. Nothing!"

THE NEWS

It was the afternoon of Saturday, the 11th of December 1999, exactly twenty years since the day when everybody in Mcuncuzo woke up to find that the Ncadana children were gone, never to heard from again. Their disappearance was now the stuff of legends. People were talking, in hushed tones, about the great tragedy that befall the house of Ncadana, when in one week the family was sucked out of life by the big winds of the great beyond.

Of course, as with every tragedy, the Ncadana tragedy also over the years generated a great deal of humour, especially among young women faced with the prospect of being married away by their families. You'd hear some of them saying, 'if my family does not cease and desist with this, I'll do a Ncadana!' And some would poke fun at Dingalethu for scaring the poor children away!

The house of Mandla and Nonzame Ncadana at Mcuncuzo was now almost obscured by overgrown vegetation, and dust and spider webs had settled on every item inside each of the three huts. In the days following the disappearance of Liziwe and her siblings, Manyawuza had made a point of coming to the house to open the doors and windows and do some dusting. But as the years went

146

by, with her age catching up with her, her visits became less frequent, and eventually she stopped coming entirely.

Manyawuza was now an old lady, having just turned seventy five years old. These days, each time when she wakes up in the morning, she would curse herself for overstaying her time on this earth. Whenever anyone greeted her, her standard response would be, 'Oh my child I don't know why God has kept me here!'

Today as she sat on a wooden bench in the front yard of her house, she was feeling sad, as usual. But today she was more so because she was thinking about Liziwe and the children, for the umpteenth time. In fact not a day had passed when Manyawuza didn't think what happened to them. Every day she had wrecked her mind trying to think what could possibly have happened to Liziwe and her siblings, where they could have disappeared to, and how they were doing today. She had tried to listen to gossip in the village about any possible sightings of the children. She had even asked her own children who were living in big cities to keep a look out.

Over the years, Manyawuza had written numerous letters to the then Radio Transkei and Radio Xhosa, requesting for an announcement of the missing children of Ncadana, and even though these announcements were read out, nothing came of them. Yet Manyawuza never lost hope, and certainly it never even entered her head that the children might not be alive anymore. She was old now, and her health was not what it used to be. She no longer ventured out beyond the yard of her house. She was content with just sitting at her house, doing little chores and listening to the radio.

But, as it was, today she was listening to an afternoon news bulletin when she heard the newsreader saying something that set her heart into a flutter of excitement. Without thinking much about what she needed to do next, she grabbed her walking stick and hurried out of her house, leaving the radio still on, all the while muttering to herself, '*oh umkhulu Bawo!*'. She was suddenly filled with this idea that she must urgently speak to MamNgwevu, herself now an elderly lady of about the same age.

When she arrived at MamNgwevu's house, which was about two houses away from hers, instead of the usual polite greeting, she just yelled, "Hey MamNgwevu! *Uyivile na lento ithethwa ngulo nomathotholo*?! Did you hear what the radio just said? *Isimanga sezimanga!*"

MamNgwevu replied, with thinly veiled sarcasm, "*Hayibo Nyawuza*! Don't tell me you rushed over here just to tell me about the lies of the wireless! You heard them saying there would be rain today! Where is that?!"

"No maan! This is serious", said Manyawuza slightly irritated. MamNgwevu, now curious, then said, "Alright, alright my friend! But you know, I seldom listen to the radio. Even today I've been very busy working in the fields. What did it say?"

"Well, switch it on, perhaps the item is on again", said Manyawuza.

The next news bulleting was going to be within the next ten minutes, and so they waited, with MamNgwevu still chuckling mischievously at this 'mysterious news of the wireless, which would cause an old lady to drag herself halfway through Mcuncuzo!' Manyawuza had just about enough of MamNgwevu's cutting humour, when at exactly five o'clock, it was news time again, and they heard the newsreader saying:

"This is Radio Umhlobo Wenene. The news is read to you by Songezo Tshotsho. In news breaking this afternoon - today, following three days of gruelling interviews by the Judicial Services Commission, the President announced the appointment of Ms Liziwe Ncadana, a lawyer with the Johannesburg based Legal Assistance Centre, as the new Chief Justice of the Constitutional Court of South Africa. Ms Ncadana is not only as the first woman to be a member of the Constitutional Court, but also the youngest to date, even more so as head of the apex court. Other appointments made by the President were that of Advocate Sisa Ngubelana as the Judge President of the Gauteng North High Court, Advocate Joseph Vikela to the Bhisho bench of the Eastern Cape Division, and Advocate Bantubonke Mlilo to the KwaZulu-Natal bench. Reaction to the news of this appointment has been overwhelmingly positive, with the entire legal profession and opposition parties ..."

At this point MamNgwevu switched the radio off, saying *"Hayi hayi* Nyawuza my battery is dying, I still need to listen to the story later!"

Manyawuza interrupted her, "Forget the story! *Kanti nje* what kind of person are you?! Did you hear what they just said? Oh my God! So Liziwe is alive and well! Yho yho yho! My friend this is big! We have to do something!"

"We?! But what can we do?!" Asked MamNgwevu scratching her head in bewilderment.

Manyawuza replied with alacrity, *"Hey wethu MamNgwevu!* Now that we know that she's alive, and we know where she is, we have to go to her!"

"What do you mean, 'go to her', like go to Johannesburg?!" MamNgwevu asked with undisguised incredulity.

"Yes, that's exactly what I mean!" replied Manyawuza.

"But where would we even know to look? Johannesburg is a very big place. God I'd hate to get lost! I've enough scary stories you know!" Said MamNgwevu.

"Well, the radio said she's the Chief Justice of the Constitutional Court. I'm sure taxi drivers know where the Constitutional Court is. They know where everything else is! We can ask them!"

"My friend", MamNgwevu looking, and with an intense, if slightly exaggerated frown on her face, at Manyawuza, and said, "I've heard rumours in the village that you're mad. But to see it for myself is disconcerting, to say the least!"

"OK, OK Ngwevukazi, I get you!" Said Manyawuza, "You don't have to be too silly about it. Maybe I'm too excited. But I don't want to die without seeing Nonzame's children again. I need to know they're alright. I need to encourage them to come home, so that they may pay proper respect to their parents. This news today is the one thing I've been waiting for since the day they disappeared. I can die after that."

"I know I'm going to regret this", said MamNgwevu looking serious, "But I don't want your ghost to haunt me for not coming with you to Egoli! So my friend, if you think this is important and we must do it, then let us go."

"In that case Ngwevukazi, time is of the essence. Let's leave first thing in the morning!"

MANYAWUZA IS IN TOWN

He pushed the driver's seat as far back as it could go, and reclined it, again as far as it could go, all the while dejectedly talking to himself, "Okay, this is falling flat now. Man, talk of an occasional gust of wind! There's nothing here anymore. Nothing. Oh well, let me take a quick nap. I'll just get a drink later, and then go home". This was Phila Nkewane, trying to come to terms with the fact that the story he'd been chasing would not develop anymore wings.

He had been a journalist on the judicial beat for as long as he cared to remember. But today, and all of a sudden, he was bored. For the past week he had been following the interviews of the Judicial Services Commission with keen interest. There was the initial excitement about who the JSC was recommending for the various bench positions in the country, especially the recommendation of the young Advocate Liziwe Ncadana. As predicted, the President had carried the recommendations as they were. But the President had added to the excitement by announcing that the highest court in the land would henceforth be led by a very young black woman. The country was taken totally by surprise at this development, because usually the leadership of the court was preserved for the longest serving judges.

But looking at her legal career, Phila became surprised that the country was surprised. It was there in black and white. At age fourteen, she obtained her Junior Certificate, and at seventeen she was a first year student at the University of Witwatersrand. At age twenty one she obtained her LLB, cum laude. After that, she was given a scholarship by Harvard Law to do an LLM, which she completed at the age of twenty three. She stayed at Harvard for her LLD, while also being mentored by a Boston based law firm. At age twenty six she returned to the country and quickly joined the Pretoria Bar of Advocates, and later she joined the Legal Assistance Centre in Johannesburg, where she became involved with numerous community level cases, most of which she handled *pro bono*. She also acted as a judge in the Constitutional Court on several occasions.

Phila had followed the news of Advocate Ncadana's appointment very closely. His views on the process were sought by a number of news outlets in the country. In fact, a day ago he had even penned a feature article in a major Sunday newspaper.

But for all the excitement in the world, the story had now died, displaced by new developments in the country. The ruling party was having an elective national conference, with the President said to be fighting the biggest political battle of his life. And so all attention and media space was now dedicated to this event.

Nonetheless, Phila lingered around the Constitutional Court with the vain hope that he might catch a break and get a new angle on the story, or for that matter a new story altogether. He knew that there were many people threatening to take a variety of matters to the court, all unrelated to the Ncadana story, and so he kept in constant touch with the court registrar, to check if anything had come in. Besides, this Liziwe Ncadana who was also proving to be something of a recluse, having refused all attempts to interview her, might just pop in at the court, Phila thought, trying to put a positive spin on things.

It was during one of these 'check-ins' that he saw these two old ladies alighting out of an Eastern Cape registered taxi. He watched as the driver just dropped them there, and then speeding of, as if not wanting to be called back.

This raised Phila's curiosity, and momentarily made him to forget about being bored and wanting a drink. For one thing, there was no hearing of any matter scheduled in court today, and the ladies also looked lost and confused. It was clear the court itself was their destination, because they kept looking at the building and tentatively searching for its entrance.

After watching them for a while, Phila decided to approach and offer assistance. "What are you looking for ladies?" Phila asked as soon as he reached them.

"We are looking for this new woman judge", said Manyawuza.

"Which woman judge is that?" Phila asked, interrupting Manyawuza in mid-sentence.

"We are looking for Lizeka Ncadana. We know her from back home", again, Manyawuza said.

"Where are you from?" Phila asked, now curious as hell. "We're from Mcuncuzo, in Cofimvaba." Said Manyawuza.

Phila was a city boy and had never been to any of the places mentioned by Manyawuza. Of course as a newshound, he had heard of the town of Cofimvaba from whence some of the country's freedom fighters had come, including Chris Hani of the South African Communist Party and Clarence

Makwetu of the Pan African Congress. In fact in his mind he started to conjure up a twisted narrative about mothers of freedom fighters whose granddaughter had achieved unimagined success!

Again, looking at the two ladies with inquisitive eyes, he asked, "So, your plan was to what, stop here and ask around?!"

"Exactly!" MamNgwevu chimed in, a touch sarcastically.

"Well! Well! well! They say these impulses are mostly prevalent among the youth. But who knew?!" Phila said, to no one in particular, and continued, just as Manyawuza and MamNgwevu were beginning to wonder about his state of mind, "Well ladies, you are in luck".

As he said this, he was already thinking that this was the best chance to finally get an interview with Advocate Ncadana. "I do have her number, and I know where she stays. I'll dial her number and let you speak with her, OK?" he said."

That will be super!" Said Manyawuza excitedly.

"Hello, is this Advocate Ncadana?" Phila asked as soon as Liziwe picked up. Liziwe of course knew Phila's number from his previous attempts to get an interview with her. "Look Mr Nkewane, I thought I made it clear that I don't want to do an interview with you at this stage, please!" She said.

Phila quickly replied, sensing that Liziwe might drop the phone, and said, "It's not about that ma'am. I have people here who are desperate to speak to you – people from home."

Liziwe's heart skipped a bit and she froze, all the while wondering who these 'people from home' might be. In all this time, since she left Mcuncuzo those many years ago, she had not had any contact with 'people from home' as this journalist was putting it. At last she said, "Well, give them the phone."

Instantly Liziwe knew who it was the moment Manyawuza said, "Hey Liziwe *kunjani mntanam*?! *Silapha noMamNgwevu!*" Before she knew it, she was crying, and instead of answering Manyawuza's question, she said, "MamNyawuza please give the phone back to the man. I want to direct him what to do."

Indeed Manyawuza handed the phone back to Phila, and Liziwe said, "Please, will you do me this favour and drive those ladies over to my house."

"A favour, you said, it's done mam. We'll be there in about thirty minutes." Phila said, and then he asked Manyawuza and MamNgwevu to get into his car, a beige Volvo S40 sedan and he drove them to Liziwe's house at number 114 Ontdekkers Road, Florida, Roodepoort.

GOING HOME

Phila Nkewane arrived in the suburb of Florida just before midday, and pulled up in front of the gate. Immediately he noticed that there was a policeman, walking up and down the yard, not far from the gate. This was a clear sign that the owner of this house was someone in authority, Phila thought.

When the policemen saw them pulling up, he opened the remote controlled gate, without asking who they were. He already knew of their arrival, again Phila noticed. As soon as they got out of the car, the policeman ushered them into the lounge.

A few minutes later Liziwe emerged from the Kitchen. She was still in her work clothes – a grey suit, with a while blouse underneath, and high heeled black shoes. She was tall and strikingly beautiful, with short hair and big brown eyes, Phila observed. She had been about to leave the house when Phila called.

When they saw her, both Manyawuza and MamNgwevu stood up. Quite why they did this Phila didn't know, but there was an irresistible aura of authority about Liziwe, which the two elderly women were instinctively picking up on when they stood up.

"*Hayini bethuna nank'uLiziwe!*" Manyawuza exclaimed, with both of her arms extended for an embrace, and continued, "Oh my God! Look at her MamNgwevu! Look at her! It's Nonzame back from the grave! And Mandla too, all in one!"

MamNgwevu just stood there, with her mouth agape, just looking at Liziwe in utter amazement. And then she said, "*Molo wethu Qwathikazi*! I'm so glad to finally see you after these years. *Bendingasoze ndikwazi*! If I ran into you in town I would not have known it was you!"

"Hey wethu Liziwe, how have you been?!" Manyawuza asked, interrupting MamNgwevu.

Liziwe did not immediately reply to anything they were asking. She just joined them in a tearful group hug. After that, she broke off and extended a greeting hand to Phila. She had a firm handshake, Phila noticed.

Phila, who had been watching discreetly, could see that this was a meeting he was not equipped to describe – it had nothing of the dry, cold and logical stuff so characteristic of legal journalism. These were deep feelings.

"Thank you Mr Nkewane. Were it not for your rather fortunate happenstance, I don't know what would have become of the two ladies. I guess we can now say that loitering too has its value! Thank you indeed." She said.

"Don't mention it ma'am." Phila said, with a wry smile responding to the joke about loitering.

"By the way, Mr Nkewane", said Liziwe, abruptly changing the subject, "I'm a judge. I don't do favours, and I seriously discourage interviews with the media, and I will not be granting you an interview today. Of course you're welcome to join us for dinner. I've arranged for all members of the family to be here tonight to welcome these two ladies and to have a braai."

Phila could take a hint. She was allowing him just a little latitude, but she was not going to be specific about anything. There was fire in her eyes, belying not only a sharp intellect but danger as well.

After her brief chat with Phila, Liziwe then returned to Manyawuza and MamNgwevu, who were whispering to themselves, and still looking at her with amazement. Looking at Manyawuza, she asked, "Mam'Nyawuza how did you guys find out where I am?!"

"*Hey wena, heee!*" said Manyawuza, "You have no idea! After years of trying to find out where you were, and then the radio just blurted it out last Saturday, that you were now a big judge! And so we decided to take a taxi to the place where judges are!" Liziwe laughed at this naïve and childlike spontaneity. It brought back memories of how she had done the same thing many years ago.

"And by the way where is Tembisa and Ntando?" Manyawuza asked.

"They will be here this evening" Liziwe said. MamNgwevu also asked, "What are they doing now? Wow they must be big now!"

"Indeed they are!" said Liziwe, and continued, "Tembisa is now a Chartered Accountant with a firm in Johannesburg. Ntando is finishing his medical studies. He'll be a doctor next year. But listen, I'll answer all your questions later tonight. I have to leave for the office. I'm still winding things up where I was. Make yourselves at home. I'm sure you're tired. The bathrooms are this side, and if you need to sleep, you'll be shown where the guest bedrooms are."

With that, Liziwe was off, together with the policeman that had been guarding her gate, a Constable Joseph Mazibuko. Phila, after a brief chat with Manyawuza and MamNgwevu, also took his leave thereafter, leaving Manyawuza and MamNgwevu in the care Liziwe's house helper, Mrs Joan Mokhehle, known simply as Marhadebe.

As Liziwe got into the passenger seat of the black seven series BMW driven by Constable Mazibuko, she was thinking about this unannounced visit by people from back home. It was an interesting coincidence, because she too had been thinking about home a lot lately. And being appointed to the Constitutional Court had the effect of making her to miss her mother. In fact when she heard the news that she had been recommended for appointment to the Constitutional Court, she became numb and was overwhelmed with emotions. The recommendation was no doubt a coronation of unceasing effort, she thought, with a deep sigh, and she wished she could go and 'talk' to her mother, to tell her to rest – that everything, and everybody was fine.

Even though she had participated in the JSC interviews process, knowing very well that there could only be one of two outcomes – to get appointed to the Constitutional Court, or not. Still, the recommendation of her appointment had taken her by surprise. At the tender age of thirty one, she had not expected that anyone had taken notice of her in this way. As far as she was concerned there were seasoned veterans in the legal field who were more deserving of the honour to serve in the country's apex court.

But the announcement made later by the President, confirming her appointment, exciting as it was, made her to be nostalgic, and she felt lonely. She thought of her mother, and how she would have reacted to the news of her success. No doubt, Liziwe thought, she would have said, 'Liziwe, make the best of it my child. *Uz' ungalal' emqokozweni!*'

The announcement also made her to go back, in her mind, to the night when she had to flee from home to search, as it turned out, for a better alternative for herself and her siblings. Today, as she watched street light poles and buildings whizzing past as the car was moving towards her office in central Johannesburg, the one overriding emotions she felt intensely was pride.

Later that evening, the house at number 114 Ontdekkers Road in Florida was buzzing with activity. On hearing the news that Manyawuza had landed in Johannesburg, Liziwe's first instinct had been to call everybody. The clan, as Liziwe and her siblings called themselves, had made plans to get together by the weekend to celebrate Liziwe's appointment. But with the arrival of Manyawuza and MamNgwevu, Liziwe decided to bring those plans forward. At about seven o'clock in the evening, Marhadebe, who had been busy cooking a storm in the kitchen and setting up the dining room table, called to say dinner is served.

When everybody had taken their seats at the table, Liziwe asked Manyawuza to say a prayer. After that Liziwe stood up and said,

> *"Bantakwethu, I have called you here for three reasons. Firstly I wanted you to all welcome my mother's friends. All of you here are children. So you do not need to know what their names are. Suffice to say that this is Mama Nyawuza, and this Mama MamNgwevu. They are from Mcuncuzo, and they arrived this morning."*

At this point Liziwe turned to face Manyawuza and MamNgwevu, and said,

"Mam'Nyawuza, Mam'MamNgwevu, oh I'm so glad to see you! Let me introduce you to everybody. This is my family. This tall beautiful thing here is my sister Tembisa. I know you know her as a small naughty child!

The big man here is my brother Ntando. Notice how big he is, and how he resembles my father!

But even more importantly, when I left home those many years ago, even though I did not know it at the time, the gods were pushing me and Tembisa and Ntando to unite with our blood. This here is my sister Lizeka. We look like identical twins, but she is two years younger than me. She is currently doing her BCom Masters at Oxford University in London, and is now home for the December holidays.

This here is my brother Phikolomzi. Notice how he and Ntando are so much alike, and I can tell you, it's not just looks – their temperament as well. He is studying mechanical engineering at the University of Cape Town.

This here is a very close family friend – someone I proudly call my other mother. This is Mrs Nomaza Makhuzeni. We call her 'mam'Zaza', and these two handsome gentlemen are her sons, Zolani and Shepard. They are all in the same school as Ntando, and they will all be doctors next year. If today we are all the things I've described, mam'Zaza's guiding hand has had something to do with it.

You all know Mr Phila Nkewane. He is a newspaper journalist, and now a friend of the family, by virtue of the fact that he found my

*mothers and brought them here to us safely. To him
we owe a debt of gratitude.*

*Secondly, I called you here to tell you that
this year we are spending Christmas at home in
Mcuncuzo. Ntandos and Phiko will organize all
the relevant logistics.*

*MamNyawuza and Mam'MamNgwevu, I
don't know when you intended to return home, but I
suggest you stick around and let us all leave in a week.*

*Thirdly, and perhaps more importantly, I have
been thinking that we need to repatriate the bodies
of Fred and Marike Le Roux, as well as that of aunt
Mavis to Mcuncuzo – to join my mother and my
father. This is a proposal I would like us to discuss,
and agree to. And if indeed we do agree, then I will
suggest that both Tembisa and Lizeka should lead
this project, especially in terms of navigating all the
legal and cultural issues attached to it. I suggest
that in December next year we should all gather at
home for the re-interring of these remains, and for
the unveiling of all the graves of our parents. By 'our
parents' I include both Marike and Fred."*

Liziwe stopped talking after this, and looked around
the table, searching for agreement. There was silence all
around, with both Manyawuza and MamNgwevu looking
at one another, their eyes wondering. Looking at them
fidgeting, Liziwe sensed what they were struggling with. She
could hear their questions: Would AmaQwathi accept the
responsibility of burying white people as their own? Would
they think it's a good idea to bury a 'side chick' alongside
the husband and the wife?

At last Ntando decided to break the uneasy silence that had descended in the room, and said,

> *"Liz, I get why you want us to do this. Of course it does seem odd, especially because all three of these people have no connection with Mcuncuzo. Nobody knows them there. The people of Mcuncuzo might object to having complete strangers, much more so to having white people being buried in their midst. I also do think that there should be more discussion with sis'Lizeka and Phiko about the reburial of aunt Mavis. She was their mother."*

Liziwe took a deep breath and then said,

> *"I hear you Ntandos. For the record, this is a consultation, and aunt Mavis was our mother – all of us. I'm therefore not going to have another private discussion with anyone. All of us are here, and all of us are going to talk here, openly. These are the three most important persons in our lives. We should at all times honour their memory, and live our own lives according to the moral standards they set. We shall never be able to repay the debt we owe to them. But putting them among our people, and holding their example of selflessness as a shrine, is the sincerest way in which we can honour them. In my humble opinion, our customs and cultural beliefs do not preclude fraternity with strangers. Of course if it will set your mind at ease, I shall immediately, as soon as we arrive at home, inform the elders of our clan fully about our intentions. Are we together?"*

There were murmurs of agreement all around the table, and then Lizeka stood up and said,

> *"Thank you Liz! I fully support this. I know it is unusual. But then there is nothing usual about my mother, and certainly there is nothing usual about Fred and Marike Le Roux. And as I have come to learn from you, Tembisa and Ntando over the years, there is definitely nothing usual about mam'Nonzame. With all of them resting in one place, it will serve to unite us as their children."*

Lizeka sat down after saying this. She was crying. Manyawuza, who had been listening intently as Liziwe and Lizeka were talking, stood up, and said,

> *"Thank you Liziwe my child for the warm welcome you have afforded us in your very beautiful house. I can't begin to describe how I feel sitting here and watching all of you. I am more than amazed that you have managed to pull all your father's children under your care and guidance like this. How I wish that all young people could learn the lesson of how to care and how to build a family from you. You have done all this without a man in your life! My friend and I agree that we can all leave together whenever you are ready to go. I'm just so excited at the thought that the children of Nonzame, who were long lost, will be returning home! I did not know the people you are talking about. But I support your idea of bringing them together. Thank you Liziwe!"*

There was spontaneous applause around the table, and when it ended, Liziwe again stood up and said, "That settles it then. Let us prepare to go home."

Phila Nkewane, who had been listening to this with more than growing interest, also stood up and said, "May I also come along? I've never been to the rural areas before."

Everybody burst out laughing, and when the laughter had died down, Liziwe, without standing as she had been doing up to this point, said, "You're not exactly family Mr Nkewane! But hey the more the merrier!"

But as Liziwe was finishing off this point, she felt a slight nudge from Tembisa's elbow, who was sitting next to her. When she looked, trying to find out what was on her mind now, Tembisa winked at her, and said, whispering, "Hey Liz, I think this one likes you! And he's cute too!" Liziwe whispered back, almost hissing, "*Pulease*!!"

Epilogue

Word quickly spread that the long disappeared children of Ncadana were back at home. The legend came to life! People were talking – that the children, now grown-ups, had come back to exact revenge! Yet still, everybody was raving about the heroic role of Manyawuza and MamNgwevu. But more than that, there was great excitement about how successful they all were. There was a lot of talk about Liziwe being a 'judge of all judges!'

In the morning following their arrival, many people from the village were stopping by to meet and greet Liziwe and her party of relatives and friends. Manyawuza, with renewed vigour, was there to introduce Liziwe's family to anyone who was asking.

Some people, on hearing that she was a 'big' judge, were not wasting any time – they wanted Liziwe to solve their problems. One complained about the local chief who had arrested him unfairly. Could the judge help? Another complained about her chicken run being broken into by thieves and a number of chicken being stolen, and the person who had done this was known in the village, but nothing was being done. Could the judge help? Yet another came with a complaint that his son was in prison for a crime he did not commit. Could the judge help? Still another one complained that even though his daughter in law had ended the marriage with his son, her father was refusing to return the lobola cows. Could the judge help?

Of course Liziwe, tired as she was from the driving from Johannesburg, would not say no. She made a list of all the complaints, with the full intention of following up on all of them. But uppermost in her mind was to have a talk with members and leaders of the clan of AmaQwathi. As soon as she was done listening to complaints, she requested Manyawuza to organize a quick gathering of AmaQwathi.

At first Manyawuza was not sure if this is a good idea. Besides, meetings of the clan were not usually called by women! But Liziwe insisted, saying, "Well Mam'Nyawuza I am calling the meeting, and I think I can assure you, they will come. Don't worry. As you know, yesterday the first thing I did when I arrived was the courtesy visit I paid to tat'uNkosini. He and I have an understanding."

Manyawuza had of course also informed her that the old man Madevu, and all the old women who were there when her parents died, had also since died, and that now the affairs of the clan were being organised and led by Nkosini, who too was frail and could hardly walk.

Liziwe then asked Ntando to drive with Manyawuza around the village so that those that need a ride can be assisted. By about midday, word had quickly spread that the judge wants to have a meeting. The village rumour mill became alive, and there were jokes galore, most of them going like, 'You stole your neighbour's chicken? The judge is here for you! That illicit affair you are having with another man's wife? The judge knows about it! You've been selling liquor without a trading license? The judge is here for you! Tonight there are many people who will be sleeping in jail!'

All this banter and humour had the net effect of completely burying the message. That this was a meeting for AmaQwathi only, became mute, as the kraal area of the Ncadana house just filled up with elderly men and women from all clans in the village. It looked like an imbizo, only called by Judge Liziwe Ncadana instead of the chief. In fact the chief himself was seen walking through the gate.

Manyawuza was horrified! "Liziwe, these people think you're here to take over from the chief!"

"Well, it doesn't matter now", Liziwe said, and continued, "Let's make a feast of it. See if you can't get us somebody who can give us four or five cows and a few sheep. I know it is short notice. But as the meeting continues I want the youth to be slaughtering and cooking."

Manyawuza looked at her, shaking her head with puzzlement, and then said, "OK ma'am, it shall be done. You sure are behaving like a chief!"

To Phila Nkewane, the city slicker, all this looked quite fascinating. There was something regal about Liziwe, and everybody approached her with unmistakable deference. Phila watched as she approached the kraal area where everybody was gathered, waiting for her. The place quickly descended into absolute silence. You could hear a needle fall. She took her seat next to the old man known as Nkosini, who promptly gestured that the meeting was now ready to start.

But just at that point, Liziwe, for a fleeting moment became horrified at seeing Dingalethu! She had completely forgotten about him all these years, and now there he was, making a late entry into the meeting accompanied by four elderly men. He was even older now, and uglier! Liziwe derisively observed.

Manyawuza saw her reaction, and quickly moved closer to her, and whispered, "Hey it looks like AmaQithi are still saying what they were saying! *Bathi ayiphel' into abayithethayo!*" Liziwe whispered back, "Well, we shall see about that!"

Old man Nkosini slowly stood up, and he said,

> "*MaQwathi! Friends, people of Mcuncuzo and guests, you are all welcome to this gathering. To my chief, Nkosi Nduneni, I say 'Ah Zweliyazongoma!' We are honoured today as AmaQwathi that our children, whom we thought we lost, are safely home. But more than that, we are honoured as the house of Mcuncuzo that we have among us, our very own judge! I will not take any more of your time than I already have. I'm an old man now. My bones are not what they used to be. So I shall sit down now. But before I do that, I will ask my daughter here, Judge Liziwe Ncadana to address you.*"

But as the old man was sitting down, and before Liziwe could speak, Dingalethu jumped from his seat, and at almost the top of his voice, said,

> "*This here is my wife! That she disappeared for all these years is of no consequence. Our union as directed by both AmaQwathi and AmaQithi still holds. As I'm sure you will all recall, even though she disappeared, I nonetheless paid her dowry in full, in lieu of my solemn commitment to the arrangement*

*made by both of our houses. I have since prepared a
home for her and I secured enough land for her to
live off of. I am therefore, together with these men
from the house of AmaQithi, here to collect my wife
and to take her home with me. She is by right the
wife of AmaQithi, oNdinga, oDlomo, oZondwa,
abaThembu."*

With this, Dingalethu sat down, huffing and puffing.
Liziwe heard Manyawuza exclaiming next her, "Amen!!"
When she saw that Dingalethu was done talking, Liziwe
stood up, panned around, making eye contact with
everybody, and then turned to look at Nkosini, and said,

*"Thank you tat'uNkosini for letting me to address
this important gathering of our people - AmaQwathi
in particular, and the whole of Mcuncuzo in general.
I will not take much of your time. I requested this
meeting for only two reasons.*

*Firstly I came home after twenty years of 'exile'
in respect, and in deference to Mam'Nyawuza and
Mam'MamNgwevu who took the trouble of going
to Egoli to look for me.*

*I came here to open my mother's house, to make
fire, to cook umngqusho, to join the women at the
fountain, to listen to the roosters in the morning.
I came here to clean the graves of my parents, to
rebuild them such that in a few months' time we
would return for an unveiling of the stones.*

*I came here to receive, together with my sister
Tembisa and my brother Ntando, the rite of
imbeleko. I came here to request you as elders of*

our clan, to conclude Ntando's rites of passage to manhood. He turned 18 at a time when we still could not come home, and so I arranged for him to get medical circumcision.

I came here to introduce to you my father's children, my sister Lizeka and my brother Phikolomzi. They all have the blood of Ncadana in them.

I came here not in triumph, but to announce to you that I have established a foundation dedicated to supporting in particular the educational needs of children who are forced by circumstances to act as head of their families, and in general, orphans in rural areas such as Mcuncuzo. The name of the foundation is called the Marike, Fred & Mavis Foundation, or the MFM Foundation for short. You do not know these people, yet you owe a debt of gratitude to them, which is why we, in consultations with the leaders of our clan, have decided to establish a memorial shrine dedicated to preserving the memory of these people, here at Mcuncuzo."

At this point Liziwe turned and faced Dingalethu. Dingalethu felt the glare, and he started to fidget uncomfortably in his seat. Looking straight and unflinchingly at him, Liziwe said,

"Secondly, twenty years ago, you were gathered here to discuss my, and my siblings' fate. I disagreed with you then, and I expressed such disagreement by doing the only thing I could as a child. I ran away. Today I'm not a child anymore. I'm a free citizen

of this country. The matter of who is, and is not my husband is my, and my decision alone. I can also tell you, as a judge in the apex court of the land, the custom of both AmaQwathi and AmaQithi does not supersede my rights as a citizen of this country."

Liziwe sat down after this. There was silence. In all the time she'd been speaking, everybody was hanging onto every one of the words coming out of her mouth. And then the silence yielded to rapturous applause, with women ululating. The old man Nkosini again slowly stood up, and said, "We have no other business to discuss. As you can see, a feast is being prepared, in which all of you here are graciously invited to partake. My children are back home. Let us celebrate!"

….The End….

List of Characters

1) Liziwe Ncadana
2) Tembisa Ncadana (Liziwe's sister)
3) Ntando Ncadana (Liziwe's brother)
4) Mandla Ncadana (Liziwe' father)
5) Nonzame Ncadana (Liziwe' mother)
6) Mrs Doreen Mokoena (Liziwe's teacher)
7) Nothembile Guluza (Manyawuza) (Nonzame's friend)
8) Dingalethu Mahomba (Liziwe's suitor)
9) Mrs Joan Mokhehle (Liziwe's house helper)
10) Constable Joseph Mazibuko (Liziwe's body guard and driver)
11) Mavis Nobahle Nxego (Mandla's girlfriend)
12) Mxolisi (Mavis's boyfriend)
13) Phikolomzi (Mavis's son)
14) Marike Le Roux (Mavis's employer)
15) Fred Le Roux (Mavis's employer)
16) Nomaza Makhuzeni (Mavis's friend)
17) Dr Van Heerden (Mavis's doctor)
18) Brian Cooling (the Le Roux's attorney)
19) Nkosini (A member of the AmaQwathi clan)
20) Madevu (A member of the AmaQwathi clan)

21) Mamanci (A member of the AmaQwathi clan)
22) Soyintombi (A member of the AmaQwathi clan)
23) Nodanile (A member of the AmaQwathi clan)
24) Manyano (Dingalethu's father)
25) Advocate Bantubonke Mlilo (Judge Candidate)
26) Advocate Sisa Ngubelanga (Judge Candidate)
27) Advocate Joseph Vikela (Judge candidate)
28) Matshaya (Security guard)
29) Reverend Dinga (Priest at the Roman Catholic Church)
30) Mrs Banzi (Principal at Mcuncuzo Primary School)
31) The Bus Conductor (Vaal Maseru Bus Service)
32) Phila Nkewane (Journalist)
33) MamQoco (village woman)
34) Nkosi Nduneni of Mcuncuzo ('Ah Zweliyazongoma)
35) Dr Hans Maree
36) Mrs Joan Mokhehle
37) Zolani and Shepard Makhuzeni